NAUGHTY AND NICE

ALEATHA ROMIG

NEW YORK TIMES BESTSELLING AUTHOR

A Brutal Vows Holiday Novella

2025 Edition License

Without in any way limiting the author's [and publisher's] exclusive rights under copyright, any use of this publication to "train" generative artificial intelligence (AI) technologies to generate text is expressly prohibited. The author reserves all rights to license uses of this work for generative AI training and development of machine learning language models. This book was 100% written by a human and did not use AI.

ALEATHA ROMIG'S MOST RECENT AND UPCOMING RELEASES

Visit Aleatha's store to purchase e-books, signed books, and store exclusive items.

RECENT RELEASES

NAUGHTY AND NICE - A Brutal Vows Holiday Novella

Marriage of convenience, Mafia/cartel romance, romantic suspense, friends to lovers, he falls first, strong heroine, possessive hero, dangerous romance

FEAR OF FLAMES - A Romantic Thriller

Suspense, Crime, Corruption, Protective hero, Strong heroine, Thriller, Mystery, Romance, Curvy heroine, dangerous romance

DEFENDING LOVE - Standalone Novel

A steamy, high-stakes, romantic suspense with body-

guard vibes, second chances, and all the feels—set in the same world as the Sinclair Duet

TO HAVE AND TO HOLD - Brutal Vows, book five - March 2025

Arranged marriage, Mafia/cartel, enemies to lovers, age-gap, he falls first, protective hero, Romeo and Juliet vibes, dangerous romance

QUEENS AND MONSTERS - Brutal Vows, book four - January 2025

Arranged marriage, Mafia/cartel, alpha hero, virgin heroine, touch her and die, family saga, he falls first, possessive hero, sheltered heroine, dangerous romance

BOUND BY A PROMISE – Brutal Vows, book three - October 2024

Arranged marriage, age-gap, forbidden, Mafia/cartel dangerous stand-alone romance

ONE STRING – July 2024

Aleatha's Lighter Ones - Second-chance, enemies-to-lovers, fake-date, little-sister's-best-friend, forbidden, stand-alone contemporary romance

TILL DEATH DO US PART- Brutal Vows, book two - June 2024

Arranged marriage, enemies to lovers, Mafia/cartel, he falls first, stand-alone, dangerous romance

NOW AND FOREVER – Brutal Vows, book one - May 2024

Arranged marriage, age-gap, Mafia/cartel stand-alone romance

LIGHT DARK – April 2024

Cult, psychological thriller, forced proximity, romantic suspense stand-alone

*Previously published through Thomas and Mercer as INTO THE LIGHT and AWAY FROM THE DARK

REMEMBERING PASSION – Sinclair Duet book one – September 2023

Scorching hot, second-chance romance filled with the suspense and intrigue

REKINDLING DESIRE – Sinclair Duet, book two – October 2023

Scorching hot, second-chance romance filled with the suspense and intrigue

For a complete list of all Aleatha Romig's works, turn to BOOKS BY ALEATHA at the end of this novel.

SYNOPSIS:

Cartel romance, marriage of convenience, slow burn, protective hero, unexpected love, independent heroine, he falls first, age-gap, organized crime, morally gray hero, widow heroine, trauma recovery, dangerous romance

As a newly declared lieutenant in the Roríguez cartel, I'm told I need a wife. The cartel allegiance with the Luciano family has mandated multiple matrimonial mergers. However, I'm not looking for a wife in the true sense of the word. Liliana Ruiz has been in my life for years. I'd never before looked at her as a woman to pursue. When I first met her, she was damaged and timid.

Time allowed Liliana to grow into not only a beautiful woman, but an independent soul. She doesn't want to marry, yet thc time will come when it isn't her choice.

Maybe I can convince her to a mutually agreeable solution: marriage in name only.

Everything changes when danger threatens the Roríguez cartel.

Have you been Aleatha'd?

Spend the holidays with the familiar characters from the Luciano famiglia and Roríguez cartel in this 34,000-word Brutal Vows novella—complete story with HEA.

*You don't need to have read the other books in Brutal Vows to enjoy NAUGHTY AND NICE.

Liliana

"Liliana," Celeste said as she pushed my office door open and stuck her head inside. "*Qué pasa?*"

I looked up at the woman I considered a friend. Today her hair was light blond with bright pink tips. Nodding, I feigned a smile. "*Estoy bien.*" I jutted my chin toward the computer screen. "I'm trying to catch up on a few things."

Celeste came in and sat on the chair beside my desk. "I thought Izzy did most of the paperwork."

"She does." I turned the screen toward Celeste. "This is something else."

Celeste's eyes widened. "Community college. I didn't know you wanted to go to college."

Pressing my lips together, I shrugged. "I've been thinking about it for a while. It was Izzy's idea." My gaze lowered. "I didn't think I was smart enough to go to college."

"Are you kidding?" Her volume rose. "Liliana, you know so much about what's happening here in the apartments. I mean, Mia is in charge, but you're the blood and soul of this place." Her lips curled. "Are you thinking about counseling? Because you're great talking with any of us."

"I was thinking about teaching." I shrugged. "Izzy asked me to put together a class for new arrivals, basic stuff." My cheeks rose. "It was fun." I shook my head. "College will never happen."

"Why not?"

I forced a weak smile. "Hey, I'm supposed to be helping you, not the other way around."

"What's stopping you from taking a few classes?"

"My parents. They disowned me after Gerardo died, when I refused to go back to their home." The bottled-up emotion created pressure in my chest. "If it weren't for Mia, I would have been forced to go back to them. If I would've gone back, they would have married me off again."

"Chica, if any of us had parents who gave a shit about us, we wouldn't be here. Besides, who cares what your parents think? Is it too late to register for the spring semester?"

The new semester would start next month. "Can I share a secret, one that I haven't told anyone?"

"Oh, juicy," Celeste said. "*Qué es?*"

"I already applied, and San Diego Community College accepted me."

Celeste's eyes opened wide. "Why all the doubt? You're in."

"I can take online classes at first, but what if I don't do well?"

"Oh hell no. You'll do great. You know Julia is in pre-nursing classes. And Luz is taking general-study courses. They have a study time in the library on Tuesday and Thursday afternoons before Wanderland opens. You could join them."

"I want to talk to Mia, but she hasn't been in the office for over a week."

Celeste scrunched her nose. "How is Mia feeling?"

"Fine. Why?"

"Oh, come on. We know she's expecting another baby. Everyone is talking about it. *El Patrón* will have two children."

Warmth flushed my cheeks. "I'm sorry. I wasn't supposed to say anything. The morning sickness is the reason she hasn't been in. I've talked to her on the phone. I know I don't have to answer to anyone, but I feel like I owe Mia so much. I'd really like her advice."

"Then go see her. You're a Ruiz, right?"

"I was, for a short time."

"It's still your last name."

I nodded.

"You've been accepted to SDCC. Talk to Mia."

My office door opened again, and Isabella Ruiz came in. Her long yellow hair was pulled up to a high ponytail. She pursed her lips. "Am I interrupting?"

"How's Em?" Celeste asked, her eyebrows dancing.

A smile bloomed over Isabella's pretty face. "Are you still after my husband?"

"A girl can dream."

Isabella laughed, her confidence on full display. "He's good. He and Nick will be by here later today."

"Oh," Celeste said, her eyebrows arching. "Nick. He's still up for grabs."

Isabella shook her head. "Lilliana, I just wanted you to know, I'm working on collecting information for the end of the year reports." She sighed. "I can't believe I've been in San Diego for nearly five months."

Her stay was only supposed to be a month, time to help Mia after Jorge's birth. An unexpected attraction with the Roríguez lieutenant Emiliano Ruiz changed everyone's plans. Judging by Izzy's smile, the change was for the better.

Isabella's focus went to the window. "It's already December. This time of year in San Diego is nothing like December in Kansas City. It's so odd to see decorations on palm trees."

Celeste stood and gave me a wink. *"Tu puedes hacerlo."*

Isabella waited until Celeste was gone and the door was partially closed. "Do what?"

"Someone's Spanish is improving."

"Understanding, not speaking. And half the time everyone talks so fast...but I'm improving." She took the seat Celeste had left. "What's going on?"

As I told her about SDCC, Izzy's smile grew.

"I think you'll be a great teacher."

"It's just..."

Izzy tilted her head. "Just what?"

"It doesn't feel real. I have until tomorrow to register for classes if I can still get any." I shook my head. "Gerardo wouldn't approve. He'd tell me I was too stupid."

"He's dead," she said bluntly. "He was a pig. Besides, Sofia is at university. He approved of his daughter attending college but not his wife?"

There was more to that story, more that I didn't want to get into. Gerardo sent Sofia away to school to separate us, another example of his cruelty. Before I was forced to marry her father, Sofia was my best friend.

I scooted my chair back, stood, and rubbed my hands over my arms. My skin felt tight as if it were shrinking. Inhaling, I tried to fill my lungs. This visceral response was what happened when my thoughts went back to my late husband. "It's difficult to explain. I mean, you're married to Em, and he's good to you."

Izzy stood and reached for my hands. "You're freezing."

Was I?

She squeezed them, sharing the warmth of her touch. "Liliana, you're beautiful. You're intelligent. You're a survivor. You're only twenty-one years old. If you want to go to school, go. If you want to do anything, do it."

Swallowing the lump forming in my throat, I took back my hands and inhaled. "Would you mind if I had José run me over to Mia's house? I won't be gone long."

Izzy pressed her lips together. "I don't mind. Tell Mia I hope she's feeling better soon. We miss her and Jorge."

Jorge was a precious eight-month-old. On some occasions, he'd join his mother at the apartments and was the star of the show. If the residents' reaction was any indication, Jorge Roríguez would be quite the ladies' man.

"I will." I took another deep breath. "I'd really like to talk to her in person."

"Go," Izzy said. "We'll be fine here."

When Mia convinced *el Patrón*, the late *el Patrón*, that I could live alone, that "alone" came with a stipulation. I wasn't actually alone. José and Renata Pérez were my staff; they came from the mansion in Sacramento. In many ways over the last two years, they'd taken the place of my parents. José was my bodyguard and driver. His wife was my cook and house manager. Unlike my parents, they supported me, keeping me company and taking me under their wings. Renata did what she could during my marriage to Gerardo. I supposed that I should be seeking their approval. I wasn't. I was heading over to speak to the woman who saved me—Mia Roríguez.

TWO

Liliana

José passed a badge beneath a scanner. The large solid gate painted white with gold filigree moved slowly to one side. When I was married to Gerardo, we lived in a well-guarded mansion in Northern California. I hated everything about it. Currently, the-second-in-command, *el Patrón's* brother, Reinaldo, and Reinaldo's wife, Jasmine, lived there with *el Patrón's* mother, Joséfina. I could only imagine the atmosphere was much improved since my imprisonment.

Entering *el Patrón's* compound was equally as intimidating, yet it lacked the Gothic feeling of dread in my old home. We drove onto a wide driveway made of bricks leading to an ultra-modern house. A pair of armed cartel guards, one on either side of the inside gate, watched, not making any attempt to conceal the long guns they had strapped over their shoulders. Once Mia's husband, Aléjandro Roríguez, became the head of the Roríguez cartel, the security level went up.

José stopped the black sedan on the bricks and stepped out of the car as the two guards began to approach. I couldn't make out their words from within the car. José must have been convincing, because the two guards nodded and retook their original spots. My driver opened my door and offered me his hand.

José opened the second gate. Most people would be intimidated entering *el Patrn's* home. Apparently, I wasn't most people. The weight on my shoulders felt lighter as I passed through the entrance and admired the landscaping. Large pavers and rocks covered the ground between the gate and house. Smaller sandstone rocks decorated the exterior of the lower level. A festive wreath hung on the front door. As we approached the house, Silas, Mia's bodyguard opened the front door.

"*Hola, Señora Ruiz,*" he said with a smile.

"*Hola, Silas. Dónde está Mia?*"

He graciously stepped back, allowing me entry.

"Liliana," Mia called from deeper within the house.

Quickly, I passed by *el Patrón's* closed office door. The living room was exquisite, decorated in shades of white with a tall slender tree decorated with colorful lights. Large glass panels were opened to the patio. Beyond the patio and pool, the Pacific Ocean glistened under the morning sunlight, sparkling as if someone scattered millions of diamonds onto the cerulean waves.

Mia was sitting at the kitchen counter with a mug in her grip. Her long hair was pulled back into a low ponytail, and her complexion was unusually pale.

"*Dónde está Jorge*?" I asked.

"Viviana took him upstairs for his morning nap." She shook her head. "He's fighting two naps." Her eyes twinkled. "He has a stubborn streak, like his father."

"And if *el Patrón* heard you say that?"

Mia laughed. "Jano would say Jorge takes after me."

"How are you feeling?"

She lifted the mug. "Viviana's tea helps. I'm sorry I haven't been into the apartments. Jano wants me to keep food down before I head back to the office." She arched her eyebrows. "Is there a problem you didn't want to talk about on the phone?"

I set my purse on the breakfast counter and took a tall stool near Mia. "Nothing with the apartments. We miss you. Izzy said to tell you hi."

Mia nodded. "*Hola* back to her. She's surprised me." Her stare met mine. "You have too. I'm so grateful to have both of you taking care of our residents."

My stomach twisted. "I came to ask you something."

She lowered the mug to the counter. "I'm concerned by your tone. What do you want to ask?"

"I'd like to take classes at SDCC."

Mia's soft laughter filled the air. "Goodness, you had me worried. You don't need my permission to take classes. You're an adult."

"*El Patrón's* permission?"

"Jano isn't his father. I'll be happy to inform him of your decision because it is your decision. What do you want to study?"

"I think I'd like to be a teacher."

Mia grinned. "You'll make a fine teacher. We could use you at the apartments if you don't decide that teaching movie stars' children in a posh private school is a better option."

"I can't think that far ahead. I wanted to start with two or three online classes."

"Do you need tuition? We can help."

I shook my head. "I have money from Gerardo." I nodded once. "Thanks to you."

"You deserved it for putting up with him."

"We both know Jano's father had other thoughts."

Mia's eyes widened. "Do we know that?" She grinned. "I think it's fitting to use Gerardo's money for an education. That's what he'd want."

It was my turn to laugh. "We know that's not true." I paused. "I've been worried about something else. It's been almost two years since Gerardo…" I took a breath. "Am I expected to eventually wed?"

Mia nodded. "I'll admit there's been talk, but Jano listens to me. He makes his own decisions, but at the same time, he sees the world differently than those before him."

"I don't think I ever want to marry."

"I understand that. I felt the same way. As you know, for a similar reason." Over the years, Mia disclosed the not pleasant details of her first marriage. "My advice," she went on, "is not to rule it out. There are good men in the cartel or the Luciano family. Not every man is like our first husbands."

We both turned at the sound of deep voices.

The door to Aléjandro Roríguez, *el Patrón's,* office opened as Emiliano Ruiz and his cousin Nick Ruiz came out. Their faces were lined with resolve, no doubt based on the subject of their closed-door meeting. With wide shoulders and muscular tall frames, they passed through the doorframe one at a time, followed by the leader himself, *el Patrón.*

Jano's gaze went past his lieutenants to Mia. "*Cómo estás*?" he asked as he made his way to his wife.

"*Estoy bien.*"

The three men entered the kitchen. If I didn't know them, they would be scary. All tall and fierce, determination in their dark eyes. Jano came to a stop behind Mia's stool. His large hands encircled her waist as he leaned down, whispering in her ear. I couldn't hear his words, but whatever he said returned a rosy glow to her cheeks. When he looked up, he saw me. "Liliana, is everything all right at the apartments?"

"*Sí*. I came to speak to Mia."

"*Bueno*, she needs company."

I turned to Em and Nick. "*Hola*."

They both smiled, greeting me in return. While I didn't know Nick as well as I knew Em, I knew deep down that they were both good men. Isabella's happiness was proof of Em's devotion. Em felt more like a brother to me than my nephew by marriage. After Gerardo was killed, Sofia and I moved into Andrés and Valentina Ruiz's home for a few months. During that time, Em and his sister Camila became the siblings I'd never had. Nick and his sister, Mireya, were friends and cousins. Nick and Em had physically matured since that time, filling out and acquiring the expressions that come with battles fought. And matured mentally too, growing and succeeding within the cartel, both of them now top lieutenants for Aléjandro's regime.

Nick laid his hand on my shoulder. "*Cómo estás?*"

"*Muy Bien.*"

His brown eyes glistened as they locked with mine. "*Sí*, it's good to see you looking happy."

"Tell them your news," Mia said.

I sucked in a breath and slightly bowed my head as all three men stared my direction. "If *el Patrón* approves..."

"Liliana," Mia said firmly.

Inhaling, I met *el Patrón's* gaze. "I'd like to take some online classes. I've been accepted at SDCC."

Jano moved his focus from me to Mia and back to me. "What will you study?"

Unimaginable relief flooded my circulation. He wasn't forbidding it. "I think I'd like to teach." I met Mia's gaze. "Either at a posh private school or maybe at the apartments."

Her lips curled upward.

Nick laughed. "Posh private school would pay better."

"*Sí*," I replied, "Money isn't what I want. I want to help people learn, to want to learn."

Viviana came down the stairs with a finger to her lips. "If any one of you wakes Jorge, you will be responsible for getting him back to sleep."

Everyone scoffed softly.

This was the side of *el Patrón* that few witnessed, accepting of my dreams and scolded by his house-keeper. Mia told me once that Silas and Viviana were with *el Patrón's* parents for years before moving to San Diego. I'd guess that meant that they knew Aléjandro long before he became *el Patrón*.

"I should get back to the apartments," I said. "I left Izzy alone." I picked up my purse and pulled out my phone. I had a text message from José. After reading I looked up. "José is running an errand for Renata." I sighed. "I guess I need to wait."

"I'm headed to that side of town," Nick said. "I'll give you a ride."

"I can't ask you—"

"You didn't," he interrupted with a grin. "Unless you're afraid to be alone with me."

A smile came to my lips. "You're not scary, Nick Ruiz."

Nick

Em nudged me in the side as I offered to drive Liliana back to the apartments. Although heat filled my cheeks, I was relatively certain the jab wasn't noticed by anyone else in the kitchen. Ever since Em had married, he'd been telling me it was time to do the same. Basically, I've told Em to shove his advice up his ass. Before Isabella walked into his life, marriage was off his radar. My plate was full with Roríguez cartel business. Wanderland was busier than ever. My father was stepping back from his duties. Or more accurately, Aléjandro was forcing him out. According to *el Patrón*, the old men had experience, but the world was moving faster than they could adapt. He saw the cartel's future in people like Rei, Em, and me.

"Would you like a sandwich for the road?" Viviana asked.

"No, *gracias*," I replied before looking at Liliana, now standing. "Unless..."

"No," she replied. "I'll eat at the apartments." She turned to Viviana. "It won't be as good as your cooking though."

Viviana smiled and nodded. "Next time."

"Thanks, Nick. I appreciate the ride," Liliana said as we walked beyond the front door to my car.

There was something different about her that I couldn't pinpoint. While she was still the same woman who'd moved into Uncle Andrés's home after Uncle Gerardo was killed, she was different. It was as if a light had been turned off inside her that now, after a few years, was glowing.

I couldn't remember Liliana before her marriage. She was best friends with my cousin Sofia, but back then, I thought of them as children. As I opened the car door for Liliana, a whiff of lilac filled my senses. Her slender ankles came into view as her dress shifted when she lifted her sandaled feet into the car. She wasn't a child any longer.

"No problem," I replied before closing the door.

Once inside the car and behind the steering wheel, I scanned Liliana's profile—her delicate features, high cheekbones, and unbelievably long eyelashes. Her subtle beauty was on display.

Maybe it was all Em's talk of marriage, but something inside me hummed in an unfamiliar way. Liliana was easily eight inches shorter than I and over a hundred pounds lighter; yet she had a strength about her, a resolve that only comes from surviving battles. I knew because I'd survived my share.

Hitting the button, I started my BMW M4. Unlike the flashy cars Aléjandro and Rei enjoyed, my classy sedan slipped in and out of Southern California traffic unnoticed. I waited for the guard to open the gate. "A teacher, huh?"

She turned, her smile radiating. "I can't believe *el Patrón* didn't bat an eye."

"Why would he?" I pulled the car through the gate and onto the road.

Liliana looked down at her lap. "I'm used to my father's—or your uncle's—reaction to any reach for independence on my part."

"Jano is about moving forward, moving the cartel forward. Mireya, Cat, and Camila went to college. Camila is still taking classes."

Liliana turned toward me, her suede-colored eyes, large and round. "Did you ever want to go on with your education, after high school?"

"I continued my education, just not the kind you're going to pursue. Every day there's something new to learn. My life was mapped out. The Roríguez cartel was my future. It still is."

"I get it. My life was mapped out for me too...until fate stepped in."

A scoff passed over my lips. "*El Patrón's* gun wasn't fate. It was what Uncle Gerardo deserved. He was a traitor."

"He deserved a lot of things," she said, turning toward the window. "Izzy was talking about how different it is here this time of the year than it is in Kansas City. The only snow I've ever seen was in the mountains."

"I don't like to be cold. San Diego is perfect." I caught a glimpse of her out of the corner of my eye. "Or would you rather be up north?"

Liliana shook her head. "My parents are in Sacramento. They've made it clear that I'm not wanted there." She squared her shoulders. "I prefer here."

My brow furrowed. "How didn't I know that? Why wouldn't your parents want you?"

"It's not important."

"It is," I insisted. "I can't imagine my mother or father casting me out—or Mireya for that matter, and Mireya wasn't born from my mother."

She turned. "I didn't know that."

A smile lifted my cheeks. "We're learning more than I expected on this ride. Mireya's birth isn't a secret. It just isn't discussed often. Now, why don't your parents...?"

"They were honored to have me married to a Roríguez lieutenant. They wouldn't listen to my pleas to stop the marriage. To them, my marriage elevated their status within the cartel." She looked down. "It didn't matter what my feelings were."

My grip on the steering wheel tightened.

"I only told my mother once what he was like...after we were married." Liliana exhaled. "She told me that my job was to obey my husband. If I'd do it better, he wouldn't..." She didn't finish the sentence.

My knuckles blanched as I gripped the steering wheel tighter.

"After Gerardo was killed," she continued, "they blamed me for his downfall. My father wanted me to be remarried right away. He considered me damaged goods. Another lieutenant would reinstate their status."

"Fuck," I murmured. "That's bullshit."

"I owe everything to Mia. She was an angel. She convinced *el Patrón* to let me stay in San Diego." Liliana turned my way. "It was when I came to live with Valentina."

"That was over two years ago. You're not the same woman."

Liliana scoffed. "I'm the same person, Nick."

"No, I've seen you at the apartments. The whores trust you."

"Residents," she corrected.

Swallowing, I nodded. "Residents. When they're at Wanderland, they're whores."

"They're sex workers. It's their profession. They chose it. The term *whore* is demeaning."

I turned with a smile. "You're different, Liliana. When you came to live with Em, you were afraid of your own shadow. You barely said two words. A second ago, you lectured me on etiquette. And more important, you're right. I'll do better."

"You should. Your father has been good to me, but he wasn't always good to the residents. They think much more highly of you."

I wasn't sure how to reply.

Liliana reached over, laying her petite hand on my arm. "Please don't tell Lieutenant Ruiz. I don't want the women punished because I said too much."

"Your compliment is safe with me."

She released my arm. In some strange way, I felt a void, missing her touch.

"We're almost to the apartments," I said. "I sent José a text message letting him know I was driving you. I'm sure he'll be back as soon as he can." I turned to her. "Do you want me to stay?"

"No. We have cartel guards. I think I'll be okay without José sitting in a nearby room, playing solitaire on his tablet."

I pulled up to the renovated school that Mia had converted into the apartments. "See, you're no longer afraid of your shadow."

Liliana smiled as she reached for the door handle. "I'm not afraid of you either. I never was."

"Really? I'm pretty frightening in a dark alley with a knife."

"Then I'll keep to seeing you in the light. Thanks again." And she was gone.

Liliana

I woke in my apartment to a commotion coming from down the hallway. The alarm sounding in Renata's voice as she called out to José sent a chill over my flesh. Hurriedly, I wrapped my robe around myself and walked briskly toward the ruckus coming from inside their bedroom. It had been about two weeks since José disappeared to run an errand for Renata. What he hadn't told me and didn't want me to know was that he'd gone to the cartel doctor due to shortness of breath. Renata shared that with me later, worried that there was more wrong with her husband.

My knuckles rapped on their door. "Renata, *estás bien?*"

The door opened. Renata was standing in her nightgown, her eyes wide. "It's José." Tears filled her eyes. "I called Lieutenant Ruiz." She wrapped her arms around her midsection. "I'm afraid."

"Lieutenant Ruiz?" There were many.

"Emiliano."

I let out a breath. *"Puedo pasar?"* I asked, motioning toward the bed where José was lying.

"Sí, he's breathing, but his pulse...it's weak. He made a loud noise." She shook her head. "No, he won't wake."

Tears prickled the back of my eyes as I stared down at José. The realization hit like a punch to the gut. Ever since I married Gerardo, they'd been there for me—both of them. Had I told them how much their constant presence meant to me?

I reached for Renata's hand. "My *madre* would tell us to pray."

She nodded. "I've been praying."

"Maybe we could pray together," I suggested.

Together, Renata and I knelt beside José's bedside. Her pleas were audible, calling out to Saint Raphael for complete healing. While I'd given up on God during my marriage, I found myself remembering the faith I was raised to believe. There were even times at the apartments when residents would ask me if I believed and if I'd pray with them.

Over time, I'd reasoned that perhaps a greater deity had heard my pleas. Instead of sending a heart attack to save me, he sent *el Patrón* and a gun along with his angel, Mia. Renata and I continued our prayers, startled when the doorbell rang.

She turned to me with puffy bloodshot eyes.

"I'll go," I said.

My heavy heart clenched in my chest as I stood and peered down at José—my bodyguard, my driver. Tightening the sash of my robe and brushing my hair over my shoulders, I hurried toward the door. A quick peek through the peephole revealed a small cartel army. I opened the door and quickly scanned the faces of the men. Em wasn't alone. Nick was with him as well as two other soldiers who looked familiar, yet I couldn't place their names. Even though it was the middle of the night, they looked as alert as they did in the daytime.

Did these men ever sleep?

The four entered my apartment in a flurry of testosterone and purpose, men on a mission.

"*Dónde está José?*" Em asked.

"He's back here," I said, leading them through my apartment.

Renata stood back while one of the soldiers assessed her husband with a stethoscope and blood-pressure cuff. I didn't know if this dangerous-looking man had medical training, but he seemed to know what he was doing. Pressing his lips together, he nodded to Em.

"We're going to take him to the warehouse," Em said.

Renata replied, "I want to go with him."

"Of course."

I reached for Nick's arm. "Is he going to be okay?"

"I don't know." He looked around as the two soldiers lifted José. "Do you have another guard here?"

"No."

"Grab some clothes. I'm taking you to the apartments."

The apartments? I wasn't thinking straight. It wasn't morning yet, not time to go to work. "Why?"

"You can't stay here without the Pérezes."

What the heck? My neck stiffened. "I'm not leaving my apartment. This is my home. I have a security system."

"How will you get to work tomorrow?"

"Uber."

Nick's forehead furrowed and his eyebrows quirked. "Liliana, I get it. You don't want to leave, but your apartment isn't safe without José."

"Send one of the soldiers back up here. He can protect me until José is better."

Nick shook his head. "There's no way in hell I'm leaving you with one of the soldiers."

"You don't trust your own soldiers?"

He scanned from my bare feet to the top of my head. "With you, alone, while you sleep...no."

What was this, brotherly concern?

I inhaled and looked at Renata's bedside stand. The clock on the top told me it was after one in the morning. "Okay, fine. We have an empty apartment. Let me pack a few things."

Nick nodded in agreement.

Despite not wanting to leave, I understood Nick's reasoning. It seemed there was always some battle, some war, or something happening with the cartel. I may be disowned by my parents, but I wasn't by *el Patrón* and the cartel. I was still the widow of a lieutenant. If a member of the bratva or a rival cartel took me...I didn't want to think about it.

I removed my robe, laying it on my bed, and pulled my nightgown over my head. I wasn't being driven to the apartments in my nightclothes. As I reached for my bra, my bedroom door opened.

My breathing caught as Nick cursed.

"Fuck..." His eyes darkened as he scanned my body, only covered by panties. "I'm...I wasn't..."

My core twisted as he stammered.

Instead of turning away, I turned toward him. The intensity and heat of his stare scattered goose bumps over my flesh, twisting my core and tightening my nipples.

"Liliana, I didn't mean to..." He took a step closer. "I didn't know you were..." His dark orbs roamed over me. "Renata and José are on their way to the warehouse." Another step brought him even closer. "You're fucking beautiful."

I shook my head and turned, slipping on my bra. Once it was secured, Nick reached for my arm and gently turned me back toward him. Lifting my face, I met his gaze.

"You're beautiful," he repeated. "I wanted to be sure you heard me."

"I heard you." I took a breath. Warmth rippled from his wide chest, only inches from my breasts. "You don't scare me."

His hands came to my shoulders, running down my arms. "I don't want to scare you." He reached for my hair. "I've never seen your hair down, stunning."

My mind was telling me to back away, but it was my body that was obviously confused. The twisting deep within me was unfamiliar. I had the sensation that my panties were damp. The urge to lean into this man was almost too strong to resist. Never in my life had I recalled having such a visceral reaction to a man. Was this the desire other women spoke about?

I took a step back, my cheeks filling with warmth.

Nick did the same, stepping back. "I'm sorry, Liliana."

I looked down and back up. "It's the same as a bathing suit."

"I'll...Let me know when you're ready to go."

Standing still, my focus lowered, noticing the bulge beneath Nick's dark blue jeans. I nibbled on my lower lip, unsure how I was feeling. Finally, he turned and headed toward the bedroom door. As he walked, I scanned from his dark hair to his broad shoulders and down to his trim waist.

Nick was so much more of a man than his uncle had been. While he was half Gerardo's age—still a decade older than me—his presence wasn't only the existence of his toned muscles or handsome face. My body reacted because I wasn't afraid of Nick Ruiz. Over the years, I'd grown to trust him.

The spark of yearning caught fire within me, smoldering beneath the surface, a foreign flame I didn't know how to tend.

I'd never ached for a man before.

It didn't matter. I'd taken my stand—to be a single widow for the rest of my life. Besides, my name was already Ruiz. And anyway, Nick Ruiz wasn't interested in me, not like that.

CHAPTER

FIVE

Nick

What the actual fuck just happened?

Leaving Liliana in her bedroom, I paced back and forth in her living room. The furniture, holiday decorations, and other surroundings were lost on me, my mind only seeing her nearly nude. I should have knocked.

Why didn't I knock?

Her slender form and tiny breasts were the opposite of what I looked for when I sought companionship. Yet they were permanently imprinted in my brain. Her long hair flowing over her slim shoulders, the dip of her neck between her collarbones, and the way her nipples darkened as they tightened were images that played on repeat. She didn't turn away from me. Fuck no. Liliana turned toward me, strong and proud.

These thoughts were insane.

Liliana was technically my aunt, or she had been.

She was also ten years younger than me.

It wasn't like we were blood related.

What the fuck?

I needed to adjust my thinking.

Em had mentioned marriage one too many times. There was no way in hell that *el Patrón* would allow me to marry my uncle's widow. Why was I even thinking that way?

"I'm ready."

I spun to find Liliana standing with a suitcase in tow. No longer only in her underwear, she was wearing a pair of jean capris and a soft pink sweater. Her long hair was plaited into a braid, and she wore flat ballet slippers on her feet.

"Liliana, I'm sorry."

She dismissed me with a shake of her head. "Like I said, it's the same as wearing a bathing suit."

"At a topless beach."

She smiled. "I'm sure you have wars to fight or overseeing to do at Wanderland. You should get me to the apartments so you can get on with your night."

Shit, Wanderland.

My mind was definitely not in the game.

I checked my phone. No messages. Diego was at Wanderland. If anything was happening that needed my attention, he would have called or messaged. "No news from Em," I said, putting my phone back in my pocket.

Liliana's smile faded and her eyes glistened with unshed tears. "José and Renata worked for your uncle. Instead of staying in Sacramento with Rei, they followed me here. I don't want anything to happen to José."

"The doc at the warehouse can take care of whatever ails you. He's patched up stab wounds and gunshots. I'm sure José will be fine." I reached for her suitcase. "Let me help you with that."

She straightened her neck and looked up at me. "I'm not a child, Nick."

"Didn't say you were." My grip tightened on the handle. "Let's go."

Liliana locked her apartment before we walked to the elevator.

I took a moment to look at the line of doorways, separated by artwork and sconces. "This is a great building," I said. "How did you find it?"

"Mia found it for me. Jano thought it was safe." She smirked. "Apparently, not safe enough to be on my own."

The elevator doors opened, saving me from answering. The truth was that I didn't want anyone else watching over Liliana, especially not a red-blooded soldier. We stepped inside.

"Garage?" she asked, before pushing the G-button. I nodded.

Once we were to the garage, I led us to my car and put Liliana's suitcase in the trunk. She settled in the passenger seat. As I sat behind the steering wheel, she remained quiet and stared straight ahead.

"Arc we...are we okay?" I asked.

"Fine."

The small hairs on the back of my neck stood to attention. From my experience with my mom and sister, fine was never fine. "Okay." I started the car.

Liliana continued her fixation on the windshield as we drove through dark and mostly empty streets.

I tried another subject. "Are you registered for classes in January?"

A smile appeared, if only momentarily. "*Sí*, they're basic freshman courses, English and algebra."

"Algebra?"

"Before Izzy came to help at the apartments, I had trouble with some of Mia's spreadsheets. I've learned a lot from Izzy. I was shocked to know what we were doing was algebra. I even like it."

"I like you. I always have," I said.

She turned with a tight-lipped smile. "I like you too. Don't worry."

"Worry about what?"

"I'm not going to expose myself to you again."

"Fuck," I growled. "You didn't. I barged in."

Liliana scoffed. "I know I'm not exactly built like the majority of the residents."

"Don't compare yourself to whores."

"Sex workers."

"Yeah," I said, "Sex workers. You're not like them."

"I'm not a virgin."

"Not the same." I remembered what she'd told me about her parents. "You were married. That doesn't make you damaged goods or whatever the fuck you said your father told you."

Liliana inhaled. "Let's just stop this conversation."

"I lied to you."

She whipped her head toward me. "About what?"

"I'm sorry to have intruded on you. I'm not sorry I saw you. You're a beautiful, strong woman, Liliana. I know you don't want to be with anyone after Gerardo. Fuck, I don't blame you. And you and I are...family."

She nodded.

"But if you ever change your mind...there's a man out there who would treat you the way you should be treated."

Swallowing, she nodded. "Let me know when you find him." She sighed. "Because if José doesn't get well soon, I'll be living in the apartments until *el Patrón* finds me a new bodyguard."

My phone vibrated in my pocket as at the same time, Liliana's phone rang from her purse.

Our eyes met, hers round and filled with worry.

I nodded toward her purse.

Her hands trembled as she pulled her phone from the depths and read the screen. "It's Renata."

I held my breath.

"*Hola*," she said into the phone. Her next word wasn't really a word, more of a gasp and a sob. "No. No. *Lo siento*."

Without thinking, I reached over, placing my hand on her knee.

"Call me when I can help," she said. "*Te amo*." She disconnected the call.

"Fuck, Liliana. I'm sorry."

I pulled up to the apartments.

Her body trembled with sobs as she lowered her face. Squeezing her knee, I longed to do more. "Liliana."

"No." She shook her head. "I need to pull myself together before any of the residents see me."

"Most of them are at the club."

"Right. You're right."

"I'll come check on you tomorrow. If you need anything, call me. I'll drive you."

"You don't need to—" She looked up at the building. "I guess this will be my home for a while."

"I'll find you a new bodyguard, one I trust."

"Thank you, but it's not your responsibility."

An absurd idea hit me. Before I could give it more thought, I spoke, "Fuck, I have a crazy idea. You can tell me it's crazy or that I'm crazy."

She looked up with puffy eyes. "What?"

"Marry me."

Liliana blinked rapidly. "Definitely crazy. Besides, you're right. I don't want to marry again."

"It won't be like that." I let out a long breath. "Ever since Em and Izzy married, he's been after me to marry. Recently, Jano entered the discussion. Being married makes me more stable. *El Patrón's* giving Em and I more responsibility...you get the picture?"

"Nick, I'm sure there are hundreds of women who would say yes." She scoffed. "Celeste is one."

"I don't think *el Patrón* envisioned his top lieutenant marrying a" —I remembered Liliana's chastisement— "sex worker."

"He also didn't envision you marrying a widow."

"*He* did."

Liliana's eyes widened. "Not the same. Mia wasn't married to Jano's uncle."

"If I could, Liliana, I'd erase every fucking memory of that pig from your mind."

She pressed her lips together. "I wish you could."

"Let me try. Think of it as a marriage of convenience. We marry. We can live in your apartment. You can take your classes and work at the apartments. You won't be stuck here until another bodyguard is found." My lips twitched. "I can trust a guard who knows you're mine."

"What about...?" She looked down at her lap.

Liliana was hardly a scared virgin. She knew what marriage usually entailed.

"Sex," I replied. "We can sleep in different bedrooms. It will get Em and Jano off my ass and help you at the same time. We like each other. Only the live-in bodyguard will know our arrangement, and I'll pay him to wisely keep that information to himself."

"I've been in one loveless marriage."

"Don't think of it that way. We have years of friendship. You didn't have that with Uncle Gerardo."

"I'm already Liliana Ruiz."

My cheeks rose. "So you won't need a new nameplate."

She shook her head. "This is crazy. *El Patrón* will never allow it."

"He will if you tell Mia it's what you want."

Liliana turned in the seat to face me. "Nick, don't you want to marry for love?"

"I don't want you stuck in a tiny apartment with sex workers day and night. Jano wants me to marry, and honestly, I'm too fucking busy to fall in love."

She patted my arm. "Talk to me tomorrow. Maybe this is a crazy dream, and we'll both wake tomorrow with clearer heads."

"No, Liliana. I thought it was crazy when it popped into my head, but it's not. Fuck, you said it yourself. If you would've moved back with your parents, you would already be married. Your family wants you married to a lieutenant. I'm a lieutenant. I'm not a stranger. I'm not Gerardo. This can be symbolic only."

"Tomorrow." She reached for the door handle.

Opening my door, I rushed to the back of the car, lifting her suitcase from the trunk. "Let me walk you to the door."

"Are you always so nice?"

"I'm not," I replied honestly. "I'm a killer for the cartel. Few people would call me nice."

"Then I guess I'm one of the few people."

CHAPTER

SIX

Liliana

I nodded at Javier, the cartel guard at the door.

"Señora Ruiz?" He appeared puzzled by my presence and suitcase.

Feigning a smile wasn't possible. "It's José." The lump in my throat grew. "He's..." I took a breath. "They believe a heart attack."

Anguish showed in his stare. "*Señora, lo lamento.*"

"I'll be staying here for the next few days until..." I wasn't certain how to finish that sentence.

"Of course. You'll be safe here. Señora Pérez?"

I hadn't thought about where Renata would stay. "I'll text her and invite her to stay with me."

Javier was a regular guard for the apartments; however, I knew he did other work for *el Patrón* and the cartel. I imagined he'd caused deaths as well as seen them. Nevertheless, his remorse at José's unexpected demise was evident. If I hadn't lived my entire life within the cartel, I might make assumptions about the men who lived in service of *el Patrón*.

I had.

I didn't.

The information would be in my office, but I didn't need to check it. I knew there were four empty apartments—bedrooms really. During the conversion, twenty apartments, each capable of housing three women were constructed. Each apartment contained a common room and a common bathroom.

We had one completely empty apartment and one with one empty bedroom. I chose the completely empty apartment. If Renata wanted to stay with me, she could. If not, I'd have more privacy. Wandering down the empty hallways, my mind was scrambled with too much information.

Had Nick Ruiz actually proposed marriage?

It wouldn't be a real marriage but a legal one.

While in my apartment, I felt something akin to passion as Nick stared at me while I was in only my panties, but that didn't mean I was ready for... I walked past numerous apartment doors. On the nameplates were the resident's first names. Those women, most if not all of them were currently at the cartel's club Wanderland. Their job was sex.

I supported their choices yet couldn't fathom what they did, day after day, night after night. Once, I'd broached the subject with Reina who works in the offices. She shrugged and laughed, saying something about how making noise encourages the men to ejaculate faster. She said she imagines a racetrack, the faster he pumps, the faster the cars were moving. Her noises were her way of cheering for the first-place driver. If she was truly into the race, his speed increased."

I'd shaken my head in a nonjudgmental way.

My experience was so completely different. My mother's advice before my marriage was to comply and submit. I'd hoped that Gerardo would have had pity on an inexperienced woman the age of his daughter. He hadn't.

To be honest, I'd only read about female orgasms. They sounded amazing in romance books. Actors on television made them out to be earth-shaking. As far as I was concerned, they were fables, fake news, or fiction—maybe all three rolled into one.

The library and dining room were dark.

My shoes clipped the floor, the clack echoing off the walls as I went to Apartment 17. Three empty nameplates told me what I already knew. This apartment was currently uninhabited. Pushing the door open, I flipped the light switch. The standard common room came into view. There was a sofa with two chairs facing a big screen television. Behind the sofa was a small rectangular table with four chairs.

Four was funny since the apartment held three bedrooms.

I went to the far bedroom, one of the ones with a window, and flipped another light switch. A standard twin-sized bed, bedside stand, dresser, and small desk were present. Lifting my suitcase to the bed, I unzipped the sides. Removing my clothes, I slowly turned, remembering Nick's stare as I did the same thing earlier.

Even without his presence, goose bumps material-ized, and my nipples hardened. Without rational thought, I lowered my fingers beneath the waistband of my panties. I couldn't think about what I was doing. I'd never done it before.

With my eyes closed, I concentrated on Nick's dark stare.

My fingers found my folds. I bit my lip, fumbling for what seemed an unobtainable goal. A gasp escaped my lips as I slowly swirled my clit. My insides tight-ened and twisted. I bounced with a newfound rhythm. One finger and then two penetrated my folds, finding my wet, silky pussy. The tightening grew almost painful. I pushed up on my tiptoes, one hand against the wall keeping me from falling as my circulation raced and my breathing quickened.

"Oh, oh..." My sounds ricocheted off the walls,

warm essence covered my fingers, and my breath eased from my lungs.

It took a minute to get my bearings. Once I did, a sad smile spread across my face. That was an orgasm. I'd finally—a twenty-one-year-old widow—had an orgasm. Guilt overtook me as my thoughts went to Renata and José.

I donned my nightgown and after washing my hands and taking care of business in the bathroom, opened my phone. There was a text message from Izzy.

"I just heard about José. I'm so sorry. You can come stay with us. Valentina wouldn't mind. Em should have brought you here."

A smile curled my lips. That was sweet of Izzy. She and Em were still living with his parents, Andrés and Valentina. While Izzy said she was ready to move away, for her and Em to have a place of their own; I suspected she wasn't. At only nineteen, Izzy enjoyed Valentina's mothering, and I was certain, Valentina loved having a daughter-in-law in-house, after her two daughters moved to Kansas City.

I sent Renata a text message.

· · ·

"I'M WORRIED ABOUT YOU. I'm staying at the apartments. The one I'm in is completely empty except for me. There's a free bedroom if you need someplace to stay."

I HIT SEND.

Despite the late or early hour, after locking the main door and the door to my bedroom, I lay in the dark as moonlight from the mostly covered windows danced in the shadows. Nick's proposal, or whatever it was, played on repeat. His solution would solve my housing problem, but I couldn't shake the feeling that it wasn't fair to him.

Nick Ruiz, top lieutenant in the Roríguez cartel deserved more than a loveless marriage. And maybe, just maybe, I did too. My self-worth was up for debate, but what if Mia was right? What if there was a good man out there who could love me?

Waking to the sound of my alarm, it took me a moment to remember where I was and why.

The happenings of last night came back to me. I reached for my phone, expecting a text message from Renata. There wasn't one.

There was one from Nick.

"I'LL BE by the apartments around noon to check on you."

. . .

I STARTED to reply that I was fine, and he didn't need to bother, but I stopped. I needed to know if he woke this morning with the realization of his crazy proposal and had changed his mind. That would be the best-case scenario. I texted back.

"I'M OKAY. I'll have the kitchen bring lunch to the offices."

SEVEN

Liliana

On my way through the building toward the office suites, I stopped by the kitchen. A dull ache in my temples sent me on a search for caffeine. It was just after 8:00 a.m., and most of the residents were still asleep. "*Hola,*" I called to Luz. She was the resident in charge of the kitchen and a marvelous baker.

"Liliana," she replied with a smile. "You're here early."

"Something happened last night." When she didn't ask, I went on. "José is gone."

"Gone?"

I nodded with a frown.

"No." Her hazel eyes opened wide. "Are you all right?"

"I'm sad but fine. It wasn't a cartel thing. It was his heart, or so they say."

"I'm so sorry."

I pressed my lips together. "I'm sad for Renata. José was a good man. For now, I'll be staying here."

"What about your apartment?"

"I haven't heard from *el Patrón*; however, last night Ni...Lieutenant Ruiz said I couldn't stay in my apartment without a bodyguard."

"After what happened last night at Wanderland, I'm not surprised."

"What happened?" I asked, my pulse kicking up a notch.

"Two soldiers from the Cabezõn cartel."

"I thought they were all sent back to Mexico a few years ago by *el Patrón's* father."

Luz lowered her voice. "Rumor has it that they were working with Herrera." Herrera was the cartel leader who took down Jorge Roríguez. "With Jorge and Herrera both gone, they want a stake back in the market. They're challenging the new *el Patrón's* power."

I let out a long breath. "It sounds like I'll end up staying here longer than I planned. What did they do at Wanderland?"

"It wasn't with any of the residents. From what I heard, there was a disagreement about a gambling debt, guns were brandished, and Roríguez soldiers escorted them from the club."

"Anyone hurt?" I asked, suddenly concerned about Nick. He was in charge of Wanderland.

Luz shrugged. "I don't know what happened to Cabezõn's men. Everyone from Roríguez is accounted for." She looked down at the stainless-steel counter covered with flour. "I'm making blueberry muffins." Her eyes lit up. "We have a new shipment of fresh fruit. Or if you're hungry now, I can make you some eggs and bacon."

"The muffins sound amazing. I thought I'd grab a glass of orange juice and a cup of coffee. I can come back when the muffins are done."

"No," she said with a smile. "Once they're done, I'll have someone bring them to your office."

"Thank you, Luz."

With my drinks in hand, I walked toward the offices, worrying if the mayhem at Wanderland would have been settled easier if Nick wasn't spending time with me. The morning sun shining through the window in my office eased my concern. Setting the glass on the corner of my desk, I took the mug to the window.

Nighttime was gone, replaced with blue skies. Sipping my coffee, I watched as a black SUV slowed and turned into our parking lot. Through the mostly darkened window, I recognized Horace, Izzy's driver and bodyguard.

A few minutes later, as I brought my computer to life, I heard the tap of Izzy's shoes on the hallway. "*Hola*," I called.

Isabella came straight to my office. "Oh, Liliana. Are you all right? I sent you a text message last night. I'm so sorry about José."

"Does Horace know?"

Pressing her lips together, she nodded. "Em called me late last night. He said he went with José and Renata to the warehouse before thinking about you. He wanted me to check on you. What happened? Did you stay in your apartment? You know, there's something happening with another cartel." Her forehead wrinkled. "You should come stay with us. Like I said in my text message, Valentina wouldn't mind. I even asked her this morning."

"I'm staying here right now."

"Here?" She pursed her lips. "Oh, we do have an empty apartment. But don't you want to leave here—and not be here day and night?"

"I want to stay in my apartment." I shrugged. "I guess I need to wait until a new bodyguard can be assigned."

"Wait," Izzy said. "You were still in your apartment when Em left with the Pérezes. How did you get here last night?"

"Nick brought me."

"Nick was with Em?"

I nodded. "Once everyone left, Nick realized I was alone. He insisted on bringing me here."

Isabella let out a sigh. "I'm glad Nick was thinking. But seriously consider my invitation. I'm sure Mia would want you too."

My phone rang.

"Speak of the devil," I said with a grin, looking at the screen. "It's Mia. She's probably only recently heard."

Izzy waved. "I'll let you two talk."

Sitting in my desk chair, I hit the green icon. "Mia."

"Liliana, are you okay? I just heard about José. We have renovations planned in one of the bedrooms for the new baby, but you're always welcome to stay here. We have other rooms."

"Thank you, Mia. I'm at the apartments right now. We have an empty unit. I've invited Renata to come here and stay with me."

"Oh...you don't know."

Aware of the tightening and prickling of my skin, I sat taller. "What?"

"Renata isn't staying in the US. José had his citizenship; Renata doesn't. With him gone, she's afraid to stay here. She still has family in San Miguel de Allende. Jano arranged transportation for her. She left this morning."

My stomach dropped. "So fast? She couldn't even stay for his funeral?"

"Liliana, I'm sure she didn't want to leave so soon. Things happened quickly."

A new rush of sadness overtook me. In a matter of hours, I'd lost both José and Renata. "I understand."

"You don't need to be working today."

My gaze scanned my desk, bookshelves, and office. "Mia, I don't know where else to be."

"Here. You can come be here."

"I-I" —I took a breath— "I want to be here. The residents make me...feel useful."

"Liliana, you're useful. You also deserve time to mourn."

"I heard something happened at Wanderland last night. Let me feel out the residents as they wake. If they need to talk, I'll be here."

"Tonight, you can sleep here," Mia said.

"I would like to go back to my apartment."

Mia lowered her voice. "I can persuade Jano on many matters. However, when it comes to women living alone without protection, he's adamant. My husband takes the responsibility for the safety of all the members of his cartel. I can't fault him on that."

"If I had a new bodyguard?"

"I'm not sure what happened at Wanderland last night. I only know Jano has been in his office with lieutenants and soldiers coming and going since before five this morning. I'm sorry, but finding you a new bodyguard probably isn't the cartel's top priority."

I swallowed a new lump of grief. Of course, I wasn't a priority. I never had been. "I'll let you know about tonight. Thank you." With my temples throbbing, I disconnected the call before Mia could say more.

"Liliana," Angel, one of the residents, said as she stepped into my doorway with a metal basket containing something hidden beneath cloth napkins. "Luz said to bring these to you while they're still warm."

Pushing the overwhelming feeling of loss down, I feigned a smile. The rich aroma of blueberry muffins filled my senses as Angel set the basket on my desk. I pulled open the napkins; the sweet scents multiplied in the air. Four large sugar-crusted muffins filled the basket. "Oh, they smell amazing."

"Probably taste better."

"Do you want one?" I asked.

"No, those are for you and Izzy. Luz would hunt me down if I took one." She grinned. "I'd better get back to the kitchen. Everyone is starting to wake. It's earlier than usual." She scoffed. "Rumors of muffins will do that."

Liliana

I'd made my way around the apartments, stopping in the dining hall and library and walking the resident hallways. While it seemed that everyone was aware of an incident at Wanderland last night, no one had firsthand experience. There were more rumors than facts. Each time someone new gave me their opinion, the disturbance was inflated. This morning, Luz said there were two men from the Cabezõn cartel.

By nearly noon, that number had tripled—six men, all wielding weapons. Even the weapons varied from knives to guns to brass knuckles and chains. My head ached from the lack of factual information.

Instead of corroboration, my mission was to ensure the residents' mental and emotional well-being.

Were they frightened to return to Wanderland?

Were they fearful of encountering Cabezõn clients?

While a few residents offered me condolences for José, his story was not the headline of the day. Each time I thought of him, I thought of Renata. If only I'd had a chance to say goodbye and tell her how much their love, devotion, and support meant to me over the last few years.

Entering the front offices, my steps staggered.

How had I forgotten Nick's text?

There he was, leaning against the far wall, his arms crossed over his broad chest. His long legs crossed casually at the ankle. Black combat boots covered his feet. Muscles stretched the armband of his black t-shirt as a swirl of tattooed barbed wire wound around his biceps to his elbow. His attention was on the ladies behind the counter, yet I didn't see the intensity in his dark stare that I'd seen last night.

My attention went to Celeste behind the counter; she was smiling from ear to ear. I heard enough of her story to decide she was recounting the harrowing night at Wanderland. "Oh, there you are," she said to me as I entered.

Nick stood tall, his arms falling to his sides. "How are you doing?"

I scoffed, afraid to answer honestly. "I've been

talking with the residents about last night. Seems you had quite the scene."

He tilted his head. "Come back to your office."

"I-I," I stammered. "I forgot to get us food. Sorry, my mind is a bit scattered."

Nick's lips curled. "I was at *el Patrón's* earlier. Viviana sent a picnic lunch."

"Oh." The idea of protein enticed me. The sugar from this morning's muffin was wearing thin.

"No offense to Luz," Nick said, "but Viviana's cooking is outstanding."

"My mouth is watering already."

Nick's eyebrows shot upward as he extended his hand. "Let's eat."

Ignoring Celeste's wide eyes at Nick's invitation, I lifted my hand to his. The warmth of his touch enveloped my fingers as I followed. On the small table near my desk was a bona fide picnic basket. Once inside the office, Nick closed the door.

I spun at the sound of the mechanism. "Do you think that's wise?"

Nick smirked. "If it keeps Celeste and Reina out, yes."

"The residents love gossip. Do you want your father to hear about his son Lieutenant Ruiz and his aunt?"

Nick's smile dimmed. "Stop saying that. You're not my aunt. You were briefly married to my uncle. That's a different thing. Besides, you've been a widow longer than you were a wife."

"Over twice as long."

Nick took a step toward me and reached for my hands. "No more aunt/nephew discussion." He lifted my hands to his lips and gently kissed my knuckles. "You're cold."

The sadness I'd tried to hide from the residents surfaced. My eyes flooded with tears and the giant ball of emotion in my throat came up with a ragged sob. "Renata's gone too," I managed to say.

Nick released my hands and stepped closer, wrapping his arms around me, and pulling me closer. My cheek rested against the soft cotton of his shirt covering his hard chest. The steady beat of his heart hammered in my ear, easing the pounding in my temples. Uncontrollably, my shoulders quaked as tears for both José and Renata coated my cheeks.

Nick didn't push or offer platitudes. Instead, he simply held me until my tears ran out.

I pushed away from him and reached for a tissue. "God, I'm sorry, Nick." At least the pressure behind my temples had lessened.

"For what?"

A snicker bubbled from my throat. "I don't know, the wet spot on your shirt. Crying like a baby over something I can't control." I spun and slapped my hands against my thighs. "For having a breakdown."

"For being honest with me." His baritone words reverberated through my thoughts.

Honest.

When was I allowed to be honest?

I was to be strong, comforting, and reliable.

Honest wasn't an adjective for who I was.

I wiped my eyes and nose. "I'm sure I look like a total mess."

Nick shook his head. The longer hair on the top of his head swayed. "You're beautiful. I told you that last night."

Unable to stay under his intense stare, I turned to the table and opened the picnic basket. "What did Viviana prepare?"

Nick was now behind me, the warmth of his body radiating to my back. "She said there's a roast beef torta and a ham torta." He reached around me and pulled two wrapped sandwiches from the basket.

"Do you think she makes her own bolillo?" The crusty white bread looked homemade.

"Viviana?" he replied with a smirk. "I'm sure she doesn't use store-bought bread for *el Patrón*."

We distributed the food. It was as if she'd packed a magic basket the way the food continued to materialize. "I'll never eat this much."

"Eat what you can."

"My father said an appetite on a woman is unbecoming."

Nick's forehead furrowed. "I don't think I've met

your father, but when I do, I'll need someone to remind me not to kill him."

Coughing, I almost choked on the delicious ham, avocado, onion, and cheese torta. "Yeah, if you meet him, please don't do that."

"If?"

My pulse suddenly thumped in my ears as I looked up to Nick's gaze. "It's okay if you didn't mean anything we said last night. I've had time to think, and I agree, it was a crazy idea."

Swallowing his bite of torta, Nick shook his head. "I've given it some thought too."

"During the altercation at Wanderland?"

"Before and after." He laid his torta on the paper. "Cartel shit is going to happen. I'd say every night, but it could be happening now, during the day. It'll require my attention. But when it isn't happening, I'd like my attention to go to you."

"Why?" I laid my torta down and stood. "Why Nick? I'm no one."

Suddenly, he was standing, all six foot five or more inches of solid muscle. His proximity was close... cornering me—an unmovable wall. My breath caught before I could remind myself that I didn't fear Nick Ruiz. My body shuddered at the movement of his hand.

Lightly, he cupped my cheek. "Liliana, I'm not my father. I'm not my uncle. I'm not Em or *el Patrón*. I, however, will not allow you to put down my friend, someone I care about."

"Your friend?"

"You. You're not no one. I rearranged my stops today to be here. I sure as fuck wouldn't have done that for *no one*."

"Do you hear what you're saying?" I asked.

"I'm saying that I like you, being with you, and talking to you."

I shook my head. "I won't sentence you to a loveless marriage. I know what that's like. You deserve—"

Nick seized my shoulders as his strong lips came down on mine.

My body froze.

Releasing my shoulders, he gently ran his hands up and down my arms. "I'm sorry if you hated that. I needed you to stop talking."

Another snicker. "Do you kiss everyone you want to stop from talking?"

"No, I usually have much more subtle ways, like brandishing my knife."

I tipped my forehead to his chest. "I'm broken, Nick. It's not your job to fix me."

"Look at me."

Slowly, I obeyed, lifting my chin until our gazes met.

"I have no desire to fix you, Liliana. I want to help you. I want you to help me. I like being with you, you, the way you are now. You're strong. You're a survivor. I recognize that in you. You don't need fixing. Maybe all you need is to know that someone is thinking about you. Someone truly cares about you."

The lump of emotion was back. "I don't understand."

"Then let me show you."

"Isabella invited me to stay with Em's family."

Nick laughed. "With Aunt Valentina and Uncle Andrs—sounds like a party."

"And Mia. She said I could stay with them."

"Where do you want to be?"

"In my apartment." My insides twisted. Honesty meant vulnerability. However, staring up at Nick, I chose that unfamiliar path. "With you," I added softly.

Nick

My pulse quickened with Liliana's response, as barely audible as it may have been. Curling my lips, I stared down into her soft brown eyes. "I'm sorry. Could you repeat the last part?"

Liliana pressed her lips together. "You heard me."

"I'm going to need you to repeat it. Not to me," I clarified. "To *el Patrón* and Mia. Everyone knows Mia's opinion on arranged marriages. If you truly want what you just said, you'll need to tell her."

Color drained from her face as she sat back in her chair. "Just because it's what I want doesn't make it right." She shook her head and pushed the rest of her torta away. "I think I've lost my appetite."

Why were women so confusing?

Taking a deep breath, I took my seat across from Liliana and decided to change the subject. "What have you eaten today?"

She looked up. "Luz made blueberry muffins."

"Did you eat them?"

"I ate one. I also had a glass of orange juice and a couple cups of coffee."

Without a word, I pushed the ham torta toward her. "I disagree with your father on many issues, but I find an appetite on a woman to be appealing. I think it's healthy. *Mi madre y hermana* eat. While I'm sure Luz's muffin was delicious, it's hard to beat Viviana's food." I took a big bite of my torta.

Liliana turned her attention to the sandwich in front of her before slowly lifting it to her lips. She didn't say a word as she nibbled slowly, making a dent. "What happened last night at Wanderland?" she asked.

"I'm sure the whor—residents have told you."

She shook her head. "No two stories are the same. I figure if anyone would know, it would be you, the lieutenant in charge of Wanderland."

"The important part of last night was that the Cabezõn cartel is back in Southern California. They're vying for Roríguez territory."

"They're testing Jano."

Taking another bite, I nodded. "He's had a fucking uphill fight since Jorge was killed. Now with Mia expecting another baby, Jano doesn't need this shit. Things seemed settled for a short time after we took out Volkov, and Herrera was eliminated."

"Those absences created a vacuum."

"They did. Jano worked to fill the void. He followed Dario Luciano's lead and agreed to work with Andros Ivanov, the pakhan of the Detroit bratva. Ivanov's men extended their bratva's territory to include what used to be Kozlov and Volkov land."

"That was supposed to take care of the bratvas. But it didn't satisfy Herrera's people?"

I shook my head. "Some wisely came to our side."

Liliana exhaled. "The rest went to Mexico and teamed up with Cabezõn."

I sat back, stretching my neck. "Maybe instead of studying teaching, you should study territorial global criminal affairs."

There was a hint of a smile. "I don't think they offer that at SDCC."

"How do you know these things? Did" —I fucking hated saying his name— "my uncle inform you on cartel business?"

Her smile disappeared. "No. He didn't think I was smart enough to understand."

"I'd disagree. You have more of an understanding than some of our soldiers."

"I pay attention. I've learned everything here." She

looked around the office. "The residents know more than they're given credit for. They listen. They have customers who exchange information for *favors*."

"Fuck, they're like a Red Sparrow network."

"The Russian sex spies?"

A laugh bubbled from my throat. "I think you're missing your calling."

"I watched the movie with Jennifer Lawrence." Her eyes opened wider. "You think I should be a sex spy?"

"No, I think you run a sex spy network here. I need to talk to Jano and Mia, but damn, I think there's a system here that we haven't fully exploited."

Liliana's eyebrows knitted together. "You want to exploit the residents more than they already are?"

I lifted my hand. "Wrong word. *Utilize*."

She plucked a grape from the container of fruit and popped it between her lips. "Choose your words wisely."

Reaching across the table, I laid my hand on hers and tried to ignore the way hers froze at my contact. Looking at where we touched back to her beautiful eyes, I smiled. "I'm choosing these words carefully. Listen closely."

Liliana nodded.

"You're beautiful, Liliana. You're brave and much more intelligent than you know. I enjoy being with you, talking to you, and when you'll let me...touching you." My gaze went back to our hands. A smile spread across my lips as she turned her hand, bringing our connection palm to palm, our fingers intertwined. "I'd like to marry you. I also think you deserve someone better than me, but I'm damn selfish, and I don't want to think of you with anyone else."

"Nick."

"Shh," I scolded. "I'm still working on choosing those words."

She inhaled and nodded.

"I'd like to take you to *el Patrón's* today to discuss this with him and Mia. You don't belong in this building twenty-four seven. And with the new threat of Cabezõn's men on the streets, you can't be alone in your apartment. I can help you."

"And I'm helping you?"

It was my turn to nod. "Our marriage will get Em, Jano, and my parents off my ass."

"Your parents..." She looked down. "Nicholas and Maria."

"Nearly two years," I said with conviction. "That's how long you've been widowed. Mia remarried after six months."

"She didn't have a choice."

"You do."

Liliana looked up, meeting my stare. "Do I?"

"I mean, it's a shitty choice. Stay here for an indefinite amount of time, move in with Aunt Valentina, move in with Mia, or marry me and we live in your apartment."

Her cheeks rose as her soft brown eyes took on a new shine. "When you put it like that..."

"What's your choice, Liliana?"

There was a sparkle to her eyes. However, it seemed as though she was trying to convince herself instead of me. "We like one another. That's more than I had before."

"I like you a lot. It could be more. Even if it's not, like you said, it's more than last time."

"My choice is—"

Before she could finish her sentence, the door to Liliana's office opened and banged against the wall. Releasing her hand, I stood, creating a barrier between her and the door, intuitively reaching for my gun.

Em stood in the doorway, eyes blazing with his hands up in surrender. "The fuck, Nick. I've been trying to reach you. Answer your fucking phone."

Lowering my gun, I tried to read Emiliano's body language. "What happened?"

"Two of our men were jumped down by the ship-yard. You and I are on reconnaissance."

"Jumped? Harmed?"

"Dead."

Holstering my gun, I turned back to Liliana and then to Em. "This place is on lockdown."

Em nodded. "Horace is taking Isabella home." He looked at Liliana. "You should go with her."

Liliana stood. "I should stay here with the residents."

I turned, facing her. "You should go with Horace."

She crossed her arms over her small breasts. "If the apartments are on lockdown, this is where I belong."

Isabella appeared behind Em. "I'll stay with Liliana."

"Fuck no," Em growled, turning to his wife. "You're safer at home."

She smiled with a tip of her chin. "Keep me safe here with Liliana."

TEN

Liliana

"Neither of you leave this building," Em said gruffly before dipping his face lower and kissing Isabella. "You're a stubborn woman."

"*Sí, jefe.* Married to a stubborn man."

Nick's stare focused on me, his jaw clenched, and the muscles pulling tight in his cheeks, wordlessly giving me the same warning Em had articulated.

"*Sí,*" I said quietly. "What about the club tonight?"

"We'll talk to *el Patrón.* You should know what to tell the whores soon enough," Em replied.

Nick spoke. "And then you can inform the residents."

They both turned and stomped away, disappearing from my office. I wasn't certain that anyone else noticed Nick's classification of the women residing in these apartments, but I did. Despite the obvious danger, his choice of one word made me smile.

Izzy's voice brought me back to present. "Did Mia invite you to stay with her and *el Patrón*?"

"She did." My thoughts were with another invitation, the one from the man who just left our presence. I walked to the window and watched as Em's and Nick's cars drove away. I turned back to Izzy. "Horace is still here, right?"

"Oh yes."

"I need to let Reina and Celeste know we're on lockdown."

"I already did. Day passes were revoked. We have two residents out, but they've been summoned to return."

"Out. Where?"

"Shopping, I believe. Martina and Darya applied for the day pass over a week ago."

I pictured the two women as they appeared when not at Wanderland. No one should be able to connect them to the Roríguez cartel. "I'll feel better when they're back."

Izzy sat in the chair near my desk. "I don't think *el Patrón* will close Wanderland. Remember last time?"

Moving to my desk chair, I sat and turned her way.

"I remember. We were on lockdown. It was your wedding night."

Pink bloomed on Izzy's cheeks. "It was."

"Maybe history could repeat itself."

Her blue eyes opened wide. "What do you mean?"

Shaking my head, I tried to find the right words. "Nick. Umm. He had an idea."

"What kind of idea?"

"It's crazy." It was then I spotted our unfinished lunch and changed the subject. "Have you eaten?"

"I had a salad from the dining room."

Pushing back my chair, I walked to the small table against the wall. "Viviana sent this food. Either we should eat it or put it in the refrigerator."

"Oh, Viviana, Mia's cook?" Izzy said, standing and coming closer. "When I lived there, I swear I gained ten pounds."

I scanned her petite and shapely figure. "You didn't gain ten pounds."

"Do you know she makes her own chipotle mayonnaise? Lola, Valentina's cook, is amazing, too." She hummed. "But Viviana is world class." Izzy picked up a knife and cut off part of Nick's roast beef torta. "I'll have a bite."

As Izzy ate, I thought about my father's assessment and Nick's about women eating. "Do you eat in front of Emiliano?"

Swallowing, she laughed. "Yes. Why wouldn't I?"

"My mother hardly ate a bite in front of my father.

She'd serve herself a miniscule portion and pick at it. Later in the kitchen, she'd eat."

Izzy scrunched her nose. "That's silly. My mom never did that."

"It's true, our parents can really screw us up."

"Valentina isn't shy about eating in front of Andrés. *El Patrón* didn't always come to dinner when I lived with Mia, but his presence didn't make a difference in her eating."

"You're right. When I was over there a couple weeks ago, he wanted her to eat and keep it down."

"Morning sickness sounds horrible," Izzy said, dropping a strawberry into her mouth.

"Señoras Ruiz," Horace said, turning our attention to the doorway. "Please come with me."

"What's happening?" Izzy asked.

"Our security picked up intruders at the perimeter of the property. I want to take the two of you to a safer location."

I was the one to speak. "Em told us to stay here."

"*Sí, señoras*. Safer *here*. Hurry."

Izzy hurried to her office. My hands trembled as I opened my desk drawer for my purse. It wasn't there. Then I recalled leaving it in the apartment unit where I'd spent the night. Instead, I grabbed my phone and caught up to Izzy and Horace in the hallway.

"Where are Celeste and Reina?" I asked.

"On their way to the shelter," Horace replied.

The shelter was a windowless lecture hall near the

back of the building. Before the structure was converted to the apartments, the room was a storm shelter with extra-thick cement walls and only two entrances/exits. Now it was tiered with rows of chairs and tables, the biggest classroom on the premises.

Izzy reached for my hand as we followed Horace through the eerily empty hallways. "Is this necessary?"

The answer came as the hallway went dark, and the sound of gunshots reverberated from a distance.

"*Sí, es,*" he said.

The darkness gave way to the strobing effect of the emergency lighting. Horace's attention was everywhere as he unholstered his gun. Shrill alarms accompanied the flickering lights.

"Back to the offices," he shouted over the alarms.

"The women," I said. "They have to be frightened."

"Now," he ordered.

He led the way we'd come. Once inside the office suite, he took us beyond my office and Izzy's, to Mia's office. "Go in the bathroom and lock the door."

The bathroom?

"We'll stop the intruders," he said confidently. "If we don't, we'll convince them that everyone present is in the shelter. Stay in here until I come for you or one of the lieutenants does."

Izzy stepped through the doorway and offered me her hand. "Come on, Liliana."

My feet wouldn't move.

"Liliana."

"No. I should be with the women. That's why I stayed."

"Come on," she demanded.

"You stay. Em doesn't want anything to happen to you." I turned to Horace. "No one will miss me if anything happens. I'm not agreeing to using the women as decoys. I need to get to them —now." When he narrowed his gaze, I added, *"Por favor."*

Horace clenched his jaw, his focus going to Isabella. "Señora Ruiz, stay here and lock the door."

Izzy nodded, taking a step back.

I hugged Izzy. "You'll be safe."

"I'd miss you."

I swallowed the lump in my throat and followed Horace. "Stay close behind me," Horace instructed.

"Sí."

He locked Mia's office and then locked the main door to the office suite. We were past the library and nearing the lecture hall when the emergency lighting cut out, leaving us in total—thicker than ink—darkness. The squealing alarms stopped. Even in the silence, my ears rang with the now-absent squeal. I reached out, trying to locate Horace. My fingers grazed his suit coat.

He reached for my hand. "Just a little farther, señora."

"Where are our guards?"

"Hopefully, keeping the intruders outside."

At the back entrance to the lecture hall, Horace used his badge to open the door.

"It was locked?" I asked. "What if there's a fire?"

"The lock keeps people out."

"And people in," I added. I reached for my badge. Shit. It was in my purse. "I need a badge."

"Where's yours?"

"In my purse in apartment 17."

Horace handed me his badge. "Lock the door from the inside."

"Thank you."

A chorus of hushes filled my ears as I opened the door and stepped inside. "I'm Liliana," I called out to the darkness.

Voices I recognized came from all directions. I imagined the layout of the room. Some voices were coming from above and some at my level. "Shh. Listen. We're safe in here. I have a key to get us out. First, we need to give our guards time to do their job."

"Cabezõn's men?" The question came from the darkness.

"I don't know," I replied honestly. "Where is everyone?" Again, voices came from all around the large room. "Please, come down here, near the lectern."

It wasn't possible for one's eyes to adjust in the total absence of light. Instead, other senses took over. Hearing became more acute. The ability to sense the warmth of another person and the scents of soap, lotions, and perfumes became distinguishable. Shoes scuffed against the vinyl flooring as the ladies made their way to the front of the room.

"Can we all hold hands?" I asked, reaching out for someone's touch. I waited a minute. "Is there anyone not holding someone's hand?"

No one replied.

"I'll start. Let's reassure our friends that we're safe. I'm Liliana Ruiz. I'm safe."

I squeezed the woman's hand to my right.

"*Yo soy* Maria. *Estoy segura.*"

"*Yo soy* Sara. *Estoy segura.*"

"*Yo soy* Julia. *Estoy segura.*"

"*Yo soy* Celeste. *Estoy segura.*"

The announcements continued, each woman sounding more and more confident. After the last statement, we accounted for fifty-four of the fifty-six residents.

"*Donde estan Martina y Darya?*" a familiar voice asked.

"Shopping," a voice I recognized as Reina's said. "I sent them a text telling them to return before Javier made us all come here."

I hoped they didn't get the text. I didn't want them coming back to whatever was happening outside.

CHAPTER

ELEVEN

Nick

"Get over there now," I ordered. Granted, the person on the other end of the call wasn't used to taking orders from me. "Papá, you're closer. Em and I are on our way. Get to the apartments."

"*El Patrón* doesn't want me there. If he did, I'd still be in charge."

My teeth ached under the pressure of my jaw. "Em and I are twenty minutes out. We were sent on a fucking diversion near the shipyard. Cabezõn's men are threatening the apartments. We have our regular guards. The more power we can get, the better."

"They're fucking whores. If Cabezõn thinks we'll sacrifice soldiers for whores, he's wrong."

"What the fuck?" I turned to Em who was now driving. We'd left my car stashed in a parking garage as soon as we heard what was happening at the apartments. My father's voice was coming through the speakers.

"Hang the fuck up," Em said. "Mí padre is en route."

"I'm on my way," my father acquiesced. "I just saw a text from Andrés."

"Go now," I said before disconnecting the call. "Fucking Cabezõn." The two soldiers they dumped were a way to lull Em and me away from the apartments.

"They're not all whores." Em's fingers blanched on the steering wheel as he maneuvered his way around the midday traffic. "Isabella is safe. I have to fucking believe that."

My thoughts went to Liliana.

Em spoke. "If Liliana hadn't said she was going to stay, Izzy would be safe at my parents'."

"They're both going to be safe. They have Horace with them, Javier, and half a dozen soldiers."

The muscles pulled tight in the side of Em's face. "How did Cabezõn find the location of the apartments?" He turned toward me. "Do you think we have traitors feeding Cabezõn information?"

"Liliana said something this afternoon about the

way the residents obtain information from clients. It probably goes both ways."

"Damn whores."

I braced myself as Em took a turn at an intersection on two wheels. "I'm not saying they said anything maliciously. They talk."

"When there isn't a cock in their mouth."

Fuck, was that the way I spoke about the residents? If it was, Liliana had every right to call me out. "It's a theory. I think *el Patrón* should consider utilizing the residents' undercover skills more than we do."

Em pressed his lips together and arched his eyebrows. "Undercover."

"Spy network, asshole. Think about something like the Russian Red Sparrows. We're struggling to determine loyalty—who is faithful to Roríguez and who's behind Cabezõn? Those women hear things. Men like to talk especially when they're showing off."

Em hit the button on his dashboard, trying to call Isabella again. The line rang twice.

"Em, oh, Em," her whisper came through the speakers.

His chest deflated as he let out a breath. "Fuck, Isabella. Are you all right? Are you safe? Where are you?"

She took a staggered breath. "Horace told me to hide in Mia's office bathroom. The door's locked, and I believe all the doors to the office suite are too."

"Can you hear anything?" he asked.

"No, it's quiet. Too quiet. The alarms were ringing, and the emergency lighting was flashing. Now nothing. Everything is dark."

"Stay there. We're on our way."

"Isabella," I said, "is Liliana with you?"

"No. She told Horace she wanted to be with the residents."

Heat boiled beneath my skin.

"Where did he take her?" I asked. "Where are the residents?"

"In the big lecture hall. It's reinforced. I don't know for sure, but I think all the women are there."

"Isabella," Em said. While the strain was evident in his expression, his voice was silky sweet, a way of reassurance. "Honey, you'll be all right. Stay there. I'm coming. I promise we're almost there."

"I love you."

"I love you. Now stay quiet."

The call ended.

Em pounded the steering wheel with the butt of his hand.

Andrés's name, Em's father, appeared on the screen.

Em answered, "*Qué pasa*?"

"Three of Cabezõn's men are down. We captured another. He's not being forthcoming with information, but from outside footage, we believe there are at least two more inside the apartments."

"Inside," we both exclaimed.

"Who do we have on the inside?" Em asked.

"Horace and Javier are unaccounted for." Andrés's voice lowered. "*Hijo, dónde esta Isabella?*"

"Mia's office, in the bathroom. Fuck, get to her."

"*Tío,*" I said. "The other women, including Liliana, are most likely in the shelter room, the big lecture hall at the back of the building. They're all our priority."

"*Sí,*" Andrés replied. "My daughter-in-law first." The call ended, filling the car with silence.

"The hell?" Em growled. "Isabella is more important than all of them."

"They're all important."

We were only minutes away.

The metaphorical wheels were turning in Em's head. He wasn't happy with my prioritization. I was afraid he'd go off half-cocked if he thought he could rescue Isabella. "I should tell you something before we get to the apartments."

"If it's about my wife being equal to whores, I don't want to hear it."

"It's about Liliana."

Em clenched his jaw and nodded.

"I asked her to marry me."

CHAPTER

TWELVE

Liliana

The sound of gunshots reverberated through the dark lecture hall. "Go," I whispered. "Hide behind the tables."

The room's design had four tiers of table rows, with a half-wall from the desks down.

Someone tugged on my arm. "Liliana," she whispered. "Come with us."

"I will. *Por favor, apurense.*"

Footsteps and shuffling filled the air.

Despite the commotion, within my ears, the thump of my pulse dominated.

Saving the residents was my number-one priority.

That didn't mean I didn't have other thoughts—like if I'd survive. I wondered what could have been with Nick. I questioned whether I ever told Mia how much she meant to me. Sadness seeped between my worries as I recalled José and Renata. Would Sofia believe that I missed her friendship, something else my brutal marriage had taken from me.

Taking a deep breath, I decided to unlock the door. My reason was that if it were locked, the intruders would assume we were hiding within. Pulling Horace's badge from my skirt pocket, I laid it over the scanner.

Nothing.

Of course there was nothing. The power was out.

What did that mean for the lock?

I was about to try the doorknob when I heard voices, deep Latino voices, barking orders. It wasn't difficult to decipher that they weren't Roríguez men. They were discussing a sweep, a search, looking for the whores. "*Donde estan las putas.*"

Did I have time to hide?

The click of the knob told me I didn't.

Instead, I plastered myself against the wall, where the door would cover me when it was opened. I held my breath as the door swung inward followed by a beam of light.

"*Salgán.*"

I said a silent prayer that no one would show

themselves. A tall man entered, only a few feet from where I stood. He wasn't looking in my direction. Instead, he was searching the room. The scent of gunpowder and perspiration assaulted my senses. The beam cut through the darkness, shining on empty chairs and long tables. Back and forth, he moved the beam to the top of the lecture hall and then down again.

If only I had a gun.

That was never something I'd even considered before—ever.

When Gerardo would rape me or beat me for whatever reason he came up with, I never wanted to kill him myself. I wanted him dead, *sí.* However, committing murder wasn't my plan. Today, to save the fifty-four women in this room, if I had a weapon, I would easily shoot.

The man walked forward and pounded his fist on the desk.

Though I stiffened at the bang, I stayed silent and hoped everyone else would too.

Silence.

As he turned, the beam of light skirted over the part of me not covered by the door. I held my breath, but the man didn't seem to notice me.

Walking toward the door, he called, "*No hay nadie aqui.*" He pulled the door closed.

My lungs burned as I released my breath and then

collapsed. My circulation stopped its normal flow, rushing to my feet. I slid down the wall, landing on my ass. The scrambling of feet reminded me of legions of mice scattering within dark subway tunnels in movies.

"Liliana."

"Celeste." I recognized her voice.

"I thought the door was locked."

"I did too. I don't know what happened."

She offered me her hand. "Where's your badge?"

Fumbling, I again removed Horace's badge from my pocket and handed it to Celeste. When she passed it before the sensor, nothing happened. "The power is out."

"Shit," Celeste said as she came and sat at my side.

While I couldn't see the women, I felt their presence. Slowly, the heightened tension eased. One by one, they made their way back to the front of the room. That was where we were all seated, on the floor, when the lights turned back on. I got up and passed the badge over the sensor. The sound of the locking mechanism engaging echoed through the room. I handed it to Celeste. "Go," I said, "make sure the other door is locked."

"You saved us," Luz said.

As the others agreed, I laid my finger over my lips. "We don't know if it's done."

Luz crawled to me and wrapped her arms around my shoulders. "You'll have muffins every day."

I leaned my head to her shoulder. "I have all of you every day. That's all I wanted."

Luz kissed my forehead. "No one has ever risked their life for me," she whispered. "Ever."

"Or me."

"Or me."

While the illumination lessened the unknown, my temples throbbed as I wondered what was happening outside the lecture hall. As time passed, the occupants became increasingly restless, some sitting at desks and others pacing back and forth. According to my watch, twenty minutes passed since the lights came on.

We all stilled and stared as the locking mechanism sounded the release of the lock.

Luz was the first. It happened so fast; I didn't have time to protest as a half dozen or more of the residents lined up in front of me. The door swung open.

"Liliana," a deep baritone voice called out.

"Lieutenant Ruiz," I heard others say.

Pushing my way through the wall of women, my gaze landed on the handsome dark stare of *my* Lieutenant Ruiz. "Nick."

The room of women faded as Nick came toward me and reached for my cheeks, pulling me against him. My body collided with his as his lips landed on mine. If we were in a movie, the room would be obscured by a thick fog while music played.

We weren't in a movie.

We had the attention of all fifty-four residents,

their whoops and hollers filling my ears as a rosy blush bloomed on my cheeks. I blinked as our kiss ended, and I stared into his dark brown orbs.

His voice was low and his tenor deep. His words were only intended for my ears. "If you were my wife, I'd turn your ass red for putting yourself in danger."

I leaned away, searching for malice or the intent to cause me harm. My search came up empty, seeing only concern and admiration in his eyes. "Is Isabella safe?"

He nodded.

"Horace and Javier?"

"We lost two at the shipyard this morning, and Cabezõn lost nearly half a dozen here today."

Taking a deep breath, I pressed my lips together, wishing that life didn't have to be about survival.

Nick looked around the room and spoke louder. "Ladies, *el Patrón* wants Wanderland half staffed tonight. He won't close for the night. He doesn't want Cabezõn to believe he's won. Twenty-five women. VIP only."

I turned toward the residents. "Volunteer only. If you don't want to go, stay home tonight."

Hands shot up around the room.

"VIP, hell yes," Julia said.

Looking at Nick, I widened my eyes. "I think we have enough volunteers."

"Go," he said to the residents. "The building is secure. Roríguez soldiers will be here with transports at four. Wanderland is opening on schedule. Your entertainment will be a little later than usual. Be ready to leave by four."

The room filled with chatter as the residents filed from the lecture hall until Nick and I were left alone.

"Seriously, what the fuck?" he asked. "You could have stayed with Isabella."

I nodded. "I could have, but if I had, the residents would have been alone." Before he could respond, I added, "Someone came in here."

"Someone?" A vein popped to life in his forehead. "In here?"

"I couldn't see him very well in the dark. He smelled of gunpowder and body odor. He had a long gun. The power was out, and he searched the room with a flashlight. Thankfully, he didn't come inside too far. He shone his light and banged on one of the tables. All the residents were quiet and hiding behind the tables."

"And you?"

I tipped my head toward the wall where I was standing. "I was so close to him. For the first time in my life, I wished I had a gun."

Nick reached for my hands and squeezed. "You're not a killer."

"I could have been. I would have been to save their lives."

"Can I please take you to Andrés's or Mia's home to spend the night *por favor*? I need to stay at Wanderland tonight. I want to do what you did." He clarified, "I want to make sure our employees are safe."

Employees.

I smiled at his choice of label. "Okay." I nodded. "Mia's."

"Tomorrow, we talk to *el Patrón* and Mia about our marriage."

THIRTEEN

Liliana

Mia met us at her front door, wrapping me in a hug. "Liliana, are you okay?"

I looked over my shoulder at Nick and back to Mia. "*Sí*, I am." We walked toward the living room.

"Nick." *El Patrón's* voice bellowed from his office. "*Ven aquí.*"

Nick nodded to me and backtracked to Jano's office.

Mia reached for my hand and pulled me out to the deck. I squinted as sunshine reflected off the crystal blue pool water and sparkled onto the Pacific Ocean. After what we'd been through in the apartments, it felt as if I'd escaped hell only to land in heaven. I took a seat at an umbrella table and sighed. "It was horrifying."

Mia sat on the chair to my side. "I've talked to Isabella and gotten messages from many of the residents." Her lips curled upward. "You're a hero."

I shook my head. "No, I'm not."

"You are. I heard about the man that came in the lecture hall."

My nose wrinkled. "He was close enough to smell."

"Honey, what if he'd known you were there?"

"I don't know. All I was thinking about was keeping the residents safe."

She laid her hand over mine. "Liliana, you're important."

I blinked, unsure if I'd heard her correctly.

"You are," she repeated. "Isabella told me what you told Horace, that you wouldn't be missed if anything happened to you."

"The fuck?"

We both spun toward the open glass doors. Nick was standing just outside the living room on the travertine patio pavers, his dark stare again laser focused on me.

"Did you say that?" he asked.

Standing, I met his gaze. "Horace was trying to get me to stay with Isabella in Mia's bathroom. He's her bodyguard. I understood. Emiliano would never forgive him if anything happened to Izzy. She needed to stay where she was safe. The women...they needed someone."

Nick's tenor slowed. "Did you say that no one would miss you?"

"I guess." I shrugged. "I think," I answered honestly. "It's all a blur."

Crimson seeped from Nick's collar up his neck and into his cheeks. The vein from before was back on his forehead. His wide shoulders tensed as he balled his fingers to fists at his side. "You're wrong." His nostrils flared as he turned and disappeared into Mia's home.

Unexpected tears filled my eyes. "Nick. I'm sorry. I wasn't thinking. Nick."

He didn't turn around.

In that instant, I would have accepted his threat to my ass. Enduring his stare, one filled with disappointment, was more painful than anything I'd endured with Gerardo.

Was it because I hated my first husband?

Or more specifically, was it because I didn't hate Nick?

And now he was gone.

Mia was at my side, reaching for my shoulders. "What's happening?"

I shook my head. "Nothing. I think I just ruined everything."

She led me back to the table. "Honey, start over. Why is Nick so upset?"

∾

EACH TIME I woke during the night, I checked my phone for a message from Nick. I had a couple from Isabella and some from different residents but nothing from Nick. Giving up on sleep, I went downstairs, careful not to wake anyone. The only illumination were the colorful LED lights on the beautifully decorated tree. By the time the sun rose, I was seated in Mia's kitchen at the breakfast counter with my third cup of coffee.

The house slowly came to life when Viviana and Silas joined me. Viviana and I spoke as she prepared for breakfast. Then she headed upstairs to help with Jorge.

My mind was filled with more questions than answers when Aléjandro, *el Patrón*, came down the stairs. He was wearing his customary black t-shirt and dark denim jeans. His boots on the tile clicked with his determined saunter as he entered the kitchen and poured himself a mug of coffee.

"*Buenos días*," he said.

He seemed almost approachable, as if he weren't fully in drug-lord mode yet.

Jutting his chin toward me, he gave a brief smile. "*Gracias*, for yesterday. I don't want to think how Mia would've reacted if Cabezõn had gotten to the residents."

My fingers wrapped around my warm mug, warding off the chill yesterday's memories revived. I smiled at his deliberate omission of the word *whores*. "If the man who came into the lecture hall had found us" —I'd been wondering about this scenario all night — "Would he have killed us?"

Holding his coffee mug, *el Patrón* leaned his tall muscular body against the counter. "*No sé.* I can't answer that for certain."

"If the situation were reversed?"

"I don't send soldiers to scare whores."

There's the derogatory term.

He pressed his lips together. "If it were reversed, if my soldiers found where Cabezõn housed his whores, I wouldn't have them killed."

"You wouldn't?" *Was my devotion to the women for nothing?*

"I'd put them to work or give them to my soldiers."

The coffee in my stomach soured. "Give them? They wouldn't be yours to give."

"Spoils of war."

"That's—that's worse."

"That's why I'd do it. Cabezõn would be upset to lose whores. He'd be furious to know they were working for Roríguez or being fucked by my men."

I couldn't let myself think about the alternative to dying. "Did anything happen at Wanderland last night?"

Aléjandro looked down at his watch. "I need to take this call."

"Wanderland?" I asked again.

"All quiet," he said as he headed toward his office.

I sighed with relief and sent a text message to Isabella.

"Could Horace pick me up at Mia's for work? I don't have a ride."

She replied right away.

"I'll see if he will. Em doesn't want me to go to the apartments today. I'm sorry."

I let out a breath, wondering why Em didn't want her at the apartments. Hadn't the danger passed?

"Horace doesn't need to get me. I'll ask Silas."

She replied.

"I'm sure Horace wouldn't mind."

. . .

I LOOKED up to see Mia with Jorge in her arms at the bottom of the steps. "Are you supposed to be carrying him?"

Mia shook her head. "The doctor said I couldn't lift over twenty pounds. He didn't say anything about me carrying over twenty pounds." She lifted her eyebrows. "It's all about finding loopholes—Viviana lifted Jorge." Her smile spread across her face as she kissed Jorge's light hair. "I'm just carrying him."

Jorge was tightly holding Mia's shoulder with his pudgy little hands as he gave me an uneasy once-over, scanning me with his father's dark eyes. I moved from the stool to the high chair and pulled back the tray. Mia set Jorge in the seat and secured the lap belt. I watched as she placed cut fruit on his tray.

"How are you doing this morning?" she asked.

"Worried."

"About Nick?"

"About the women. Aléjandro said the club was quiet last night, but Em doesn't want Isabella at the apartments today. I don't know what to think."

"Think that Roríguez men, whether Roríguez or Ruiz, are notoriously overprotective." As Mia made herself a cup of tea, she continued. "You surprised me with your story about Nick yesterday." She looked up as she fiddled with food for Jorge. "Do you think you could marry again?"

"I don't think it's any longer an issue. I messed it up."

"Let's say you did. Does the loss of the possibility upset you or is it a relief?"

Sighing, I leaned back against the tall stool. "More upsetting than I predicted."

"You want to marry Nick Ruiz."

"I don't know. I'm confused. He was talking about marriage, and I think I fell into a stupid fairy tale. It's ridiculous because we both know that marriage can be a nightmare, not a fairy tale."

"Jano isn't Rocco. Nick isn't Gerardo." She shrugged. "I mean, I didn't really know your late husband, but what little I did know, I detested."

My cheeks rose as I curled my lips. "Me too." I took a sip of my coffee. "Nick is different. When Sofia and I lived with Em's parents, he spent a lot of time there with Em. I got to know him. I was too confused at that time to think of him as a man. I guess I got to know him as a person. If that makes sense."

Mia nodded. "And now?"

Warmth filled my cheeks. "I've noticed he's a man." I shook my head. "More importantly, he doesn't frighten me. Even yesterday when he was upset, I wasn't scared. I didn't think about that until I was lying awake last night."

She smiled. "Jano can be intense, but I know that no matter what happened, he'd protect me, not harm me."

"Intense is a good word. Nick was upset with me." I brought my phone to life. "I keep hoping he'll message, but he hasn't." I looked up. "Do you think Silas could drive me to the apartments?"

"Really, Liliana, after José, Renata, and yesterday, you should take a few days off. I know it's winter, but the patio is still beautiful. Relax under an umbrella. Read a book."

Jorge dropped a banana slice onto the floor and giggled.

Her offer was tempting, but not going into the apartments felt a little like hiding from the issues at hand. "I want to be sure everyone is okay. And I assume tonight Wanderland will be back to full staff."

Mia wiggled her eyebrows. "The men will be."

I shook my head.

"Silas will drive you when you're ready."

FOURTEEN

Liliana

The residents were resilient and strong. Over the last eighteen months, I ventured to guess that I learned more from them than the other way around. When I entered my office, there were fresh strawberry muffins on my desk. Celeste and Reina were already present in the front office. They told me that there were too many women who volunteered for VIP last night. The ones who didn't go got together and had a movie night. Their choice of show made me laugh—*Pretty Woman.*

I didn't mention what *el Patrón* said about alternatives to being killed. The idea of being kidnapped and forced into prostitution instead of going into it will-ingly sent chills over my flesh.

It was almost as if yesterday never happened. Even our guards were quiet, not offering updates regarding Cabezõn's men. However, the word from the residents who worked last night was that two of Cabezõn's men were detained for questioning. I wanted to reach out to Nick but was too frightened that he wouldn't answer or text me back.

Compared to yesterday, today was downright jubilant. The energized residents spent the morning decorating the dining hall for the impending holidays, constructing and decorating a tree and stringing colorful lights. Carols bellowed from someone's phone.

I helped with the decorations as lunchtime approached and checked in with the residents who worked Wanderland last night. Everyone said the same thing. The night at the club was uneventful. I was sitting at a table unwinding garland when my phone buzzed with a text message.

I inhaled, nibbling my lip when I saw the name—*Nick*. Holding my breath, I read the message.

"GET *your ass to your office in five minutes or it will be* *red.*"

. . .

There was nothing about that message that should make me smile. Yet my lips curled, and warmth filled my raised cheeks. I pressed my thighs together at the sudden twisting in my core.

"Are you all right?" Julia asked. "You look...excited or scared or both."

I scoffed. "I-I need to go see someone."

"Would that someone be Lieutenant Ruiz?" she asked in a singsongy voice.

Pressing my lips together, I quickly nodded. "I thought he was upset with me."

"Girl, the way he looked at you yesterday in the lecture hall was like he wanted to eat you for dinner. I don't think you could possibly upset him."

"We're just friends." Even the idea of marriage was meant to be for show.

"You keep telling yourself that."

I stood, pushing away from the table. "Just friends."

Excitement and dread created an intoxicating concoction circulating throughout my bloodstream. By the time I made it to the office suite, my palms were moist and my breathing shallow. Opening the main door, I met with Celeste's and Reina's wide stares. "Lieutenant Ruiz?" I managed to ask.

"He's in your office. He said once you arrive, you're not to be disturbed."

I took a deep breath. "How did he seem?"

The two women exchanged glances.

"Intense," Reina finally answered.

Intense.

That was the description Mia used about her husband.

Wiping my palms on my skirt, I approached the door and reminded myself that Nick Ruiz didn't frighten me. He was nice.

Was that really an accurate description of a lethal cartel lieutenant?

Gripping the doorknob, I turned it and pushed the door inward. My mouth went dry and my breathing hitched. I closed the door behind me.

A vase with a bouquet of roses sat on the table. A picnic basket was near the table on the floor. But my attention went to the man waiting for me. Nick stood with his fine ass leaning against my desk. His arms crossed over his wide t-shirt-covered chest, his dark eyes staring down at his wristwatch. Slowly, his deep brown orbs moved upward, scanning me, inch by inch, from my ballet flats to my plaited hair. My nipples tented my blouse as he studied each place in between. A smile threatened his scowl. "You came precariously close to missing the deadline."

Swallowing, I took a step toward him. "I'm sorry about yesterday."

"I want you to be."

My stomach twisted. "You want me to be?"

He nodded, standing tall.

"You want me sorry?" I wasn't computing his words.

"Very sorry." He came closer, his cedar scent filling my senses.

It was then I noticed my desk, the black leather snake lying on top. Not a snake. It was his belt. Reddened ass. My nerves kicked into overdrive. I took a step back as if the leather could strike on its own. "If you think you have the right to punish me..."

"You made it in time."

"If I hadn't?" My voice rose an octave.

"I told you in my text message."

I squared my shoulders. "I've lived through one abusive marriage. I'm not doing that again."

"No, *tesoro*, you're not."

Tesoro—treasure, something or someone of value.

Nick didn't blink as he took another step toward me.

As much as I wanted to stand my ground, I found my feet moving backward. Each step he took forward, I took one back until I ran out of room. My shoulders collided with the wall. "Nick?" I didn't know what I was asking, but I was asking.

He came to a stop in front of me, his one hand going to the wall, caging me, while his other came gently to my chin, his calloused thumb caressing my cheek.

I stared into the depths of his dark orbs.

His deep voice reverberated through my shattered

nerves. "I don't want to marry you to get Em and Jano off my ass."

I swallowed. "You don't want to marry me." My nostrils flared. "I understand. I'm damaged."

He forcibly lifted my chin, pinching it between his thumb and finger. "I want to marry you, Liliana. I don't give a damn about pleasing Em or Jano. I want to marry you because I want you to be mine. I don't give a fuck about your past. You're not spoiled. You're a fighter, and I want to feel the heat of the fight that burns deep inside you. It's a fight to survive, to live, and to love. I want to feel it every fucking day of my life. I want to fall asleep next to you and wake up beside you."

"You said no sex."

"I've changed my mind." His palm slid to my cheek as his lips crashed down on mine.

His kiss was possessive, firm, and bold, the striking of a match igniting buried embers I'd thought were long dead. I lifted my hands to his chest; his heart drummed beneath my touch. The hard planes of his body pressed against me, yet my only thought was that I'd never been kissed like this before.

Never.

Ever.

It was intoxicating and suffocating at the same time, like a supernova, a powerful explosion setting off detonations throughout my nervous system.

Nick splayed his long fingers in the small of my

back, pulling me closer, flattening my breasts as his erection prodded against my stomach. My head snapped back as he twisted my braid. The nerves sent electricity from my scalp to my nipples, turning them from hard to diamonds and flooding my core.

He took a step back as I panted for air. "I fucking want you, Liliana. You've been right in front of me for years, and I finally opened my damn eyes." His thumb ran over my lips as he grinned. "I like seeing your lips bruised from my kiss. I want to see the way your skin reddens as I lick and kiss you."

I met his gaze. "You don't scare me, Nick Ruiz."

He dipped his head, his lips coming to the sensitive skin of my neck. The whoosh of his breath filled my ears. "Like here."

Goose bumps bloomed over my arms and legs as he nuzzled and licked.

"And here." His lips lowered down my chest.

I reached for his cheeks, my palms pushing with all their might. When he relented, his eyes met mine. "Marry me first."

"Is that a yes to my proposal?" he asked.

"Yes, Nick. It's a yes."

"This won't be in name only, Liliana. I want you to know that you're important to me. You mean something to me. You're not alone, and you would fucking be missed. I'd burn down the damn world for you."

Tears filled my eyes. "I don't...deserve—"

Nick's finger came to my lips. "You deserve more than I can ever give you."

"Sex?"

His grin broadened. "Gerardo doesn't get to live rent free in your head any longer. I'm fucking evicting him this minute. You're not afraid of sex." He inhaled and smiled. "*Tesoro*, I smell you. You're wet. Tell me I'm wrong."

My chin lowered as more warmth filled my cheeks.

Again, he lifted my chin. "Tell me."

"You're not wrong." Peering over his shoulder, I saw his belt on the desk. "I won't be in another relationship like I was before."

Nick must have followed my line of vision because he turned toward the desk and back to me. "I'm not my uncle."

"But...punish? I'm an adult, not a child."

The fire simmered in his orbs. "I'm well aware that you're a grown woman." He took my hand and lowered it to his blue jeans. "I don't get hard for a child." Releasing my hand, he kissed my forehead. "I like to be in control, Liliana. I've watched you. Submission isn't foreign to you. I promise, nothing will be nonconsensual as long as you obey my one rule."

"One? What?"

"Know that you're loved and cared for." He lifted my hand to my chest, placing it over my heart. "Know in here. The residents, Mia, Izzy, and me."

Is he saying he loves me?

Nick went on, "Never tell anyone that you won't be missed or aren't important. Know your worth, your value. Because to me, you're priceless."

My chin lowered as I dropped my forehead to his chest. My words came out muffled. "I'm not worthy of your love."

Nick wrapped his arms around me and held me tight. "You are, and that's your one and only pass on breaking my rule. From now until forever, I won't tolerate you thinking or saying otherwise."

When I looked up, tears slid down my cheeks. "I'll do my best to change my thoughts. It may take some time."

His smile bloomed. "That's what we have—time. In the meanwhile, I'll enjoy my handprint on your ass when you forget."

I shook my head, surprised by how appealing his threat sounded. Maybe there was some truth to the idea of enjoying Nick's naughty side. "I might do it on purpose."

Nick's laugh filled the office. After a quick kiss, he led me to the table. The sweet scent of roses filled my senses.

Once I sat, he crouched down and opened the picnic basket. "What's this?"

"What?" Before the word was fully out, my focus was on the diamond ring in his grasp. "Nick?"

Still on one knee, he asked the question I'd never been asked before.

"Liliana, will you do me the honor of being my wife?"

FIFTEEN

Liliana

After we ate the lunch Nick packed, I said goodbye to Celeste and Reina. "If you need anything, call. Mia told me to take a few days off, and I think I'm going to listen to her." While I was certain they had a thousand questions about what happened in my office, with Nick standing at my side, they didn't ask. "I'll be back on Monday."

Since it was Thursday afternoon, that wasn't much time away. Hopefully, the apartments had seen all the excitement they would for a while. Besides, Christmas was at the end of next week.

The engagement ring was currently in my skirt pocket. I reasoned that we needed to have Mia and *el*

Patrón's blessing before we made a public announcement.

In Nick's car on our way to Mia's home, he reached over and squeezed my knee. "Don't be nervous."

"Did you ask *el Patrón* before you asked me?"

"Technically, you and I spoke about it first."

Tightness formed in my chest.

"However, I did ask...this morning."

"And he said yes?"

"Remember when you told him about SDCC?"

I nodded.

"Similar reaction. Not a yes, not a no. He nodded and asked questions about soldiers on the street."

I laid my head against the soft leather headrest. "I can't believe it's that easy. Last time—"

"Last time," Nick interrupted, "there were negotiations with your father. Señor Socorro Cervantes forfeited his ability to speak for you. Jano is going to ask you if you want to marry me."

"You know my father's name?"

Nick laughed. "*Sí*, and your mother's, Nailea. You know my parents' names."

"I do." Looking down at my hands, I thought about my parents. "My parents will be happy I'm married." I turned toward Nick and smiled. "And to a lieutenant."

Again, he squeezed my knee. "What relationship you choose to have with them is up to you. I'll support you whether they're a part of our lives or not. You just can't ask me to honor and respect people who would treat you the way they have."

"I get it. I don't think I respect them any longer. What about Lieutenant Ruiz and Maria? Do they know?"

"*Madre* does."

My stomach twisted. "And?"

His cheeks rose with his smile. "She's very happy."

"But you haven't told your father?"

"I will. Let's make it official first."

"The ring..." I began. "It's gorgeous. Is it an heirloom?"

"No." He looked my way. "It's brand new. Like our marriage will be."

A smile spread over my face.

When we made it to *el Patrón's* gate, Nick placed his badge beneath the sensor. The large white gate with gold filigree moved slowly to the side. The armed soldiers were at their posts. Once we parked, Nick opened my door and offered me his hand. "Once we have Jano's blessing, we'll move forward."

There were other cars parked on the property. From my experience that meant that *el Patrón* was busy with business. Our marriage discussion would need to wait. With cartel business, our concerns weren't high on *el Patrón's* priority list.

"Señora Ruiz," Silas said as he opened the door. "I would've been happy to pick you up and drive you here."

"Thank you."

Nick spoke from behind me. "I'm taking care of Señora Ruiz from now on. *El Patrón*?"

"In a meeting. I'll let him know you're waiting when he's free."

"Mia?" I asked.

"Out on the patio."

Nick followed me through their home, past the closed door of Jano's office, into the kitchen that radiated with the aroma of something Viviana was preparing, through the living room past the tall decorated tree and out to the patio.

When Mia saw us coming, she laid down her book and sat up on the lounge chair. "You decided to take my advice and take some time away from the apartments?"

I sat on the chair to her side, facing her. "A couple of days. The residents are acting as if yesterday never happened. They're decorating for the holidays."

"Oh good. I asked Em to take the decorations over from the warehouse."

Mia pushed her sunglasses to the top of her head, looked up at Nick and back to me. "Is everything all right between the two of you?"

My gaze went to Nick who nodded. Reaching into the pocket of my skirt, I brought out the beautiful solitaire diamond ring. Warmth filled my cheeks as I showed it to Mia. "I said yes."

"Oh," she squealed, her fingers going to her lips.

Next, she dove forward, wrapping me in a hug. "You said yes." She looked up at Nick. "You asked Liliana, like a real gentleman."

"*El Patrón* asked you, *sí*?"

"He did after my betrothal was already arranged with Dario. I still thought Jano was a pig. So, I said no." She laughed. "That's another story. And I've changed my mind about him. I'm so happy you asked Liliana."

"Liliana is an independent adult." He smirked. "I couldn't think of anyone else to ask for her hand."

Mia stood and reached for Nick's hand. "I'm so happy." She inhaled. "Thank you. We're going to get the cartel into the current century eventually." Mia turned to me. "Why aren't you wearing that beautiful ring?"

"We need *el Patrón's* approval."

She squinted her eyes. "That move to the current century is going to take longer if we don't all push for it. Put on the ring. You said yes."

I did as she said, slipping it over the knuckle of my left fourth finger as Nick had done earlier in the day. Splaying my fingers, I looked down at the magnificent diamond. "This one makes me happy."

Nick reached for my shoulder and squeezed.

"Let's get some lemonade and celebrate," Mia said. "We have a wedding to plan." She stood. "How long of an engagement are you two thinking?"

Nick and I exchanged glances. He was the one to speak. "No more than six hours."

"What?" Mia asked. "No, no, no. Family will be in to Sacramento next week." She waved her hand. "Rei and Jasmine's home is big enough for everyone. Joséfina, Catalina and Dario, and Camila and Dante will be there. Uncle Carmine and Aunt Giulia are even coming for Isabella." Her eyes widened. "Your parents and Mireya," she said to Nick. "Valentina, Andrés, Em, and Isabella. That would be the perfect time to have a wedding."

Suddenly, I stood, unable to sit still as my blood chilled. "No." I looked up at Nick, feeling my cheeks pale. "I don't want to be in that house—mansion—prison." I reached for my hands, willing them to stop shaking. "Please, can we marry here?"

An expression of concern clouded Nick's features. "Yes."

"Oh shit," Mia said. "I obviously wasn't thinking. After you talk with Jano, we'll call for Father Gallo. I think I have him on speed dial."

We all turned as *el Patrón* came out onto the patio, carrying Jorge. "Look who I found," he said to the baby, "*tu mamá*." He kissed Mia before handing Jorge to her and turning to us. "Silas told me you're here." His dark stare and rock-hard expression came to me. "I've spoken to Nick. Now I speak with you."

Mia's hazel stare encouraged my word choice.

I took a deep breath. "*El Patrón*, Nick asked me to marry him. I said yes." I extended my left hand. "I hope you'll give us your blessing."

Jano peered toward his wife, his lips curling. "Mia, it seems we have another wedding. Do you think we can fit that into the schedule?"

Parting my lips, I exhaled.

"Tomorrow," Mia said. She turned to her husband. "That way they'll be married by the time of our family gathering."

"I still don't..."

She laid her hand on my shoulder. "Come, let's talk."

SIXTEEN

Nick

"This is what you want, no?" Jano asked as Liliana, Mia, and Jorge walked back into the house.

I watched Liliana walk away, my gaze lingering a bit too long on her round ass. I turned back to *el Patrón*. "I want the marriage very much. It's weird because it isn't like I just met Liliana. It's more that I finally saw her for who she is. I opened my fucking eyes."

"Your parents are onboard?"

"My mother. I haven't told my father. I was waiting for the final word from you."

Jano nodded. "*Tu padre's* attitude is…"

Bad.

Upsetting.

Not specifically loyal.

There were many possible ways to finish that sentence. I replied, "He's hurt. He thinks he still belongs in charge of Wanderland and the territory. He's not ready to take orders from his son."

"He takes orders from me and Reinaldo, Jorge Roríguez's sons."

I nodded. Reinaldo was Jano's brother who oversaw Northern California.

"My decisions are not negotiable," he said.

"I stand by your decisions, *el Patrón*. Liliana does as well. It's why we came here first, instead of to my father."

"We still can use Nicolas, if he can accept his new role."

Asking what the alternative would be wasn't something I planned to do. My father raised me to respect the order of the cartel and the word of our leader. Change was difficult—the loss of Jorge and committing to Aléjandro. My father taught me that the alternative was death as a traitor. Uncle Gerardo met that fate. I hoped my father wouldn't choose the same end.

"Come to my office," Jano said. "Em's on his way over, and we need to discuss Cabezõn's men. Em's been persuasive, yet they're still not talking. I want to know how they learned about the apartments." He turned to me. "Will Liliana still work with the residents?"

"She cares too much about them to even suggest she stop."

His lips curled. "The Roríguez cartel needed new thinkers. Now let's figure out how to keep our wives safe as they do the work they enjoy."

As we stepped into the living room, I saw Liliana and Mia sitting at the kitchen breakfast bar and walked toward them. They were discussing a menu with Viviana.

"...I don't want anyone to do too much work," Liliana said.

Mia saw me and sat taller. "Nick, a wedding is a special occasion. Who do you want to have present?"

My hand went to Liliana's slender shoulder. "My bride."

Mia exhaled. "You're not being helpful."

Liliana craned her neck to look up at me. "We haven't talked about it. Do you want a big celebration?"

"I want you to be my wife. If it's only the two of us and Father Gallo, I'm okay with that."

Liliana nibbled her lip. "I'd like to ask Em and Izzy to stand up with us." She reached out to Mia. "And for you and *el Patrón* to be present." She sighed. "Nicolas, Maria, and Mireya should be invited."

"We can invite Joséfina, Rei, and Jasmine," Mia

said, "but with the holidays, current cartel emergencies, and Jasmine's pregnancy, I'm not sure they can make it down from Sacramento by tomorrow." She looked at Liliana. "What about Sofia?"

"Same thing," Liliana replied. "She's in Sacramento. I'm not sure if her semester is finished."

"Do you want to invite her?" Mia asked.

My fiancée shrugged. "I don't know how she'll feel."

"Your parents?" Mia asked.

"Would you contact them?" Liliana asked. "Let them know it's happening. The choice to attend is theirs."

"Nick," *el Patrón* called.

I leaned down and kissed Liliana's cheek and whispered. "Don't forget my rule. I love you."

Her soft brown eyes sparkled as she smiled my direction. "I love you, too."

For a moment, I simply stared at Liliana's beauty, understated and regal. Her delicate features and petite frame were her disguise. Liliana wasn't fragile or weak. She was a phoenix who had risen from the ashes, now a magnificent creature, capable of anything she set out to do. Her thick crown of long dark hair framed her lovely face. I imagined the scene a few days ago in her apartment when she was nearly nude, and her hair was flowing over her shoulders.

The wedding couldn't happen soon enough.

I made my way down the hallway. Pushing Jano's office door open, I was met by Em's snarky smile. "*Hola.*"

He came my way, wrapping an arm over my head and pulling me down. "You proposed without telling me you did it." He released me and laughed.

"I told you I wanted to ask her." I scoffed. "I don't recall you telling me before you proposed to Isabella."

"Oh fuck, she's going to be so excited. I should call her."

"Or maybe you could let Liliana do that. She'd like to ask if the two of you will stand up with us."

"Of course."

El Patrón cleared his throat. "Now that the vital information is shared, maybe we can talk about more important things." He held up his hand. "No offense, Nick. We have a budding war happening."

"No offense." There was always the prospect of war, war, or war recovery. It was a vicious cycle.

Em and I sat in the chairs opposite Jano's desk.

"Rei volunteered to speak with Cabezõn's men." He lifted his eyebrows. "Em, you're good, but Rei is one of the best at interrogation. I spoke with Dario Luciano..." *el Patrón* began.

Dario Luciano, the boss of the Kansas City Famiglia and *el Patrón's* brother-in-law, was the person who first pursued an alliance between his organization and the Roríguez cartel. Those negotiations began with Dario's father, Vincent, and Jano's father, Jorge. Over the years the alliance has grown, despite the two original leaders no longer being around.

Aléjandro and Dario were determined to keep it going for the betterment of both organizations.

SEVENTEEN

Liliana

I woke in the same bedroom I'd been in the night before. Unlike the night before, I'd slept much better. Rolling on the cool sheets, I realized I was smiling, actually smiling. Today was my wedding day. Lifting my hand from below the blankets, I stared at the ring on my fourth finger.

The large round-cut diamond on a platinum band was simple, elegant, and new. No one else had ever worn it before. I gave the rings from my first wedding to Sofia. They'd first belonged to her mother, and she deserved to have them. Offering me a dead woman's jewelry should have been the first red flag in that marriage.

Yesterday afternoon, after receiving *el Patrón's* blessing, Nick and I went to the county clerk's office at Waterfront Park. While the sign said we needed a prescheduled appointment, Nick spoke with the person at the desk and arranged for us to be seen. I hadn't thought about proving Gerardo's death. Thankfully, Nick had. He had Gerardo's death certificate with him. After answering a few questions and paying a fee, we had our marriage license.

When we left the clerk's office, Nick handed me the death certificate. "He's gone now. Your last name will no longer be his but mine."

I folded the certificate and placed it in my purse.

Nick reached for my hand, and I leaned into his shoulder. "I'm proud to have your name."

He kissed the top of my head.

Next, we went to his parents' home, his home. Maria Ruiz met us at the door. I tried to read if she was truly happy, and I wanted to believe she was. She made a comment about it finally being time Nick wed. At one point, she laced her arm through mine and whispered that she'd raised a good man. This would be a much better union. I wanted to believe her.

Lieutenant Ruiz, Nick's father, was less gregarious about our announcement. I sensed he and Nick were having some issues but decided not to ask.

Looking up at the ceiling, I faced the fact that today was my wedding day. While my name wasn't changing, it was. This was a new beginning, despite the old feelings trying to creep into my mind, reminding me of my first marriage.

What did Nick say?

He said he officially evicted Gerardo Ruiz from my thoughts.

I doubted putting that part of my life behind me would be that easy, but if Nick could proclaim it, I could try to live it.

A knock came to my bedroom door.

Hurrying from the bed, I wrapped my robe over my nightgown. I made it to the door on the second knock. Opening the barrier, I found Viviana. "*Hola.*"

"*Hola,*" she said with a smile, carrying a tray with coffee. "Lieutenant Ruiz is downstairs. I didn't want him to see you today, so I brought you coffee. What can I get you for breakfast?"

"Viviana, that's a silly tradition."

"It's a tradition. After your breakfast, Mia has a surprise for you in her bedroom."

"This was supposed to be a no-fuss wedding."

"I'm sorry, have you met Señora Roríguez?"

A giggle came from my chest. "I have. Mia never does anything small."

"I made molletes, but if you'd like something else—"

"With your homemade bolillo?" I interrupted. "*Sí, por favor.*"

I'd barely made it out of the bathroom and was standing at the window overlooking the ocean, drinking my coffee, when Mia knocked and entered the bedroom.

"I'm sorry," she said, "I promised Viviana I'd let you have an easy start to your day, but I can't wait another second."

"For what?"

"Come to my room."

I stood to follow. "*El Patrón* isn't in there, is he?"

"Oh heavens no. He's downstairs in some major war council."

"War?"

Mia shook her head. "Sorry, no. It's what I call it when he has the lieutenants and top soldiers together. It's honestly a weekly event."

Okay, she scared me.

Leaving my coffee on the table, I followed.

"I confess to sneaking into your bedroom yesterday afternoon to learn your dress size."

"My dress size?"

"You're getting married, and you should do it in a new dress."

"Mia..."

"Come, they're hanging in my closet."

"Plural?" I asked.

"Don't worry. I'll send the ones you don't want back. Heaven knows I can't wear them." She opened the closet door.

It was like walking into another room. I'd say it was small, but in all reality, I think my entire bedroom in my apartment was smaller than her closet. I stopped moving upon seeing the three gowns on display. "Mia, I can't accept—"

"I know you've been married before. Big wedding. I get it. If I had more time, today's ceremony would be more. The very least you owe to yourself is a gown that makes you feel as special as you are to Nick." She tilted her head. "Please try them on."

Nick's rule came to mind—I wasn't to think of myself as unworthy.

"Okay." I nodded with a smile.

I stood in front of a full-length mirror turning slightly from side to side. This was the third gown I'd tried, and I loved the way it hung from my shoulders from thin spaghetti straps. They were attached to a sweetheart neckline, and the silk gown was formfitting. Three bows on my back were held in place by fabric-covered buttons and separated by cutouts. Lower, fabric covered a long row of hidden eye hooks. As Mia fastened the back of the dress, she said, "Oh, Nick will want to rip these buttons and eye hooks."

My smile fell.

She reached for my shoulders. "He won't, honey. I know what you're thinking. Be honest with Nick. He knows a little about what you endured. Jano and I didn't have intercourse for nearly a week after we were married."

I turned. "You told him no."

Mia lifted her eyebrows. "I did. And more importantly, he listened. But Jano and I didn't know one another at all. It was different. You and Nick know each other."

"We do," I said with a nod. "When he kisses me, I feel things I've never felt before."

She lifted her hand to her lower stomach. "A twisting?" Her hands moved higher. "Your breasts feel heavy and your nipples bead."

Heat filled my cheeks, and I lifted my hands. "Yes, that's exactly what happens."

"You never felt that before, ever?"

I shook my head. "I don't think I want to say no. I just want to...I don't know how to explain it."

Mia laid her hands on my shoulders and turned me toward the mirror. "You want to be with a man you trust. Do you trust Nick?"

There was no hesitation in my answer. "I do."

She smiled over my shoulder into the reflection. "You're gorgeous in this gown. It was designed for someone with your slender figure. Oh, I have a pearl drop necklace that would look amazing—something borrowed."

Blinking, I willed my tears to stay at bay. "I love the dress." I turned and hugged Mia. "I love you. Thank you for always being so supportive."

"The best thanks is seeing you happy." She gathered my hair. "How do you want your hair?"

EIGHTEEN

Liliana

Isabella was with me, preparing for the wedding in Mia's bedroom. "I can't wait for Nick to see you," Izzy said, excitement bubbling from her being. "You're stunning."

I'd decided on the dress with the spaghetti straps. Earlier in the afternoon, after I had a long shower, Izzy arrived. Mia had a team of makeup artists and hairstylists invade her bedroom. My dark hair was pulled up on the sides, the length cascading down my back filled with loose curls. I rarely wore it down, but I remembered what Nick had said about my hair the day in my apartment.

By the time they were done, Izzy and I looked as if we could walk the runway of a fashion show.

I scanned my friend. She was wearing a soft peach-colored satin gown. Izzy said it arrived at her house this morning with a note from Mia. Her long golden hair was piled high on her head. Teardrop diamonds dangled from her ears. "You're beautiful." I reached for her hand. "Thank you for standing up with me."

"Thank you for accepting me when I first arrived in San Diego. You're my first and best friend here." She lowered her chin in a shy smile. "I know you've been married before. So tonight won't be a surprise."

"I didn't enjoy my first wedding night. I'm hoping I will tonight."

"Nick is Em's cousin and his best friend. Em was gentle with me at first. I can't imagine Nick being different."

"Thank you." Her words registered. "At first?"

It was Izzy's turn to blush. "Let's just say we've advanced beyond vanilla."

"And you're okay with the other flavors?"

Her laughter filled the bedroom. "Yes."

We both turned to a knock on the door. "Liliana," Mia called.

"Is it time?" Izzy asked as she went to the door. I couldn't see the other side. "Oh, hi." Izzy pulled the door farther open. "You must be here to see our bride."

Tears threatened my makeup as Sofia entered the bedroom.

"Lily, you're gorgeous."

Wrapping my arms around my midsection, I stared at the woman who had been my best friend since childhood. "I didn't think you'd come."

"Jasmine contacted me. She offered me a plane ride. I didn't want to miss my best friend's wedding, the one she really wants." Sofia took a step closer. "You do want this, don't you?"

Swallowing, I nodded. "I do."

"Then I'm happy for you."

"Oh," I turned to Izzy. "Isabella, this is Sofia Ruiz. We've known one another forever. And Sofia, this is Izzy, my friend. We work together."

"Nice to meet you," Izzy said.

"Nice to meet you." Sofia took a deep breath. "I better get back downstairs."

I reached for Sofia's hand. "Thank you for coming. How are you?"

"I'm good. We should catch up. I'm going to stay with Aunt Valentina for a few days before heading back north."

"That's where I live," Izzy said.

"Oh, you're Em's wife."

"I am," Izzy replied.

"You said Jasmine is here too?" I asked. Jasmine was married to *el Patrón's* brother, Reinaldo.

"Jasmine, Rei, and Señora Roríguez. The patio is filled with people."

My eyes opened wider. "This was supposed to be small."

Izzy laughed. "Then you shouldn't have put Mia in charge."

"Lily," Sofia said, "thank you for inviting me. You didn't need to."

"I was afraid you couldn't make it, but I never questioned inviting you."

She stepped forward and hugged me. "I've always loved you. I'm sorry about so much."

I shook my head. "It was out of both of our control. Love you."

Izzy rubbed my shoulder as Sofia left the bedroom. "She was your best friend and your stepdaughter?"

"Yeah, it was totally messed up." I took a deep breath. "I'm relatively certain Nick doesn't have any children. If he does, he hasn't mentioned them."

"Not yet," Izzy said as she made her eyebrows dance.

The next knock was accompanied by a deep voice. "Liliana, it's time."

Izzy's blue eyes widened. "Is that *el Patrón*?"

"Yep. I asked him to walk me down the aisle."

She clenched her teeth. "You're one brave lady." Izzy reached for her bouquet of green holly, red roses, and ivory cream calla lilies, a smaller version of mine.

"Do you have Nick's ring?" I asked.

Izzy showed me the platinum band on her thumb

as she walked toward the door. "I'll see you downstairs." She nodded. *"El Patrón."*

The leader of the Roríguez cartel entered the bedroom. Instead of his customary dark denim jeans and a black t-shirt, he was dressed in a custom dark suit with a red shirt and black tie. "It's your last chance to change your mind."

I lifted my bouquet. "I appreciate the offer, but I'm not changing my mind."

He was actually handsome with his gelled hair and striking smile. If this was the side of Aléjandro that Mia saw, I understood why she was so head over heels in love with him.

He crooked his elbow. "Shall we?"

I placed my hand on his arm. Together, we walked to the staircase. Even from the second floor we heard the music resonating from down below. Izzy was first to descend the staircase. We followed to the landing, and I watched as Izzy disappeared from sight through the living room.

El Patrón patted my hand. "You're marrying one of my best men, but he's the one getting the best prize."

I started to say that I wasn't a prize, and then I remembered Nick's rule. "I think I'm the one winning."

"I married a widow, Liliana. There's no greater joy than when the woman you love learns to love you back despite the darkness in her past."

"I hope someday people will look at me and see the love I see coming from Mia."

"I already do." He nodded. The music changed. "*Vamos.* That's our cue."

When I made a similar walk with my father years earlier, I had the sensation of being a convicted felon walking to her execution. As I walked beside *el Patrón*, my sights were on a future to be shared with a man I liked, one who didn't frighten me, and one I believed I loved.

Sofia was right about the number of chairs and people present. I didn't try to see faces or register who was in attendance or absent. My insides twisted with the beautiful world Mia and Viviana created. Tiny white lights twinkled from around the patio and pool. Beyond the terrace, a sky filled with orange and crimson hues met with the aquamarine of the Pacific Ocean. The faint scent of sea filled my senses as the setting sun neared the horizon, and music came from hidden speakers.

The closer we walked, the less I noticed the decorations. My complete attention was on the handsome man at the altar beneath a trellis. The man in a dark suit, white shirt, and white tie. A red rose was attached to his lapel, and his dark stare was laser focused on me. Emiliano was smiling at Nick's side, and to the other side of Father Gallo was Izzy, her smile ear to ear.

"Who gives this woman?" Father Gallo asked.

"With honor," *el Patrón* said, "it is I." He placed my hand in Nick's.

I stared up at the dark brown eyes that only a few days ago were filled with rage. Today, they radiated the opposite. His adoration filled me with an unfamiliar sense of value. Nick Ruiz—a top lieutenant and a man of worth—wanted me to be his wife. *El Patrón* said he was one of his best.

"You're gorgeous, *tesoro*," Nick whispered, his deep baritone tenor sending shivers down my spine.

With my hand in Nick's, we turned toward Father Gallo.

"Liliana Cervantes Ruiz and Nicolas Ruiz, have you come here to enter into marriage without coercion, freely, and wholeheartedly?"

"We have," we said in unison.

I'd answered the same during my last wedding, but it had been a lie, not the first and not the last.

Today's answer was freeing and truthful. I was entering this marriage without coercion, freely, and wholeheartedly.

While I'd witnessed countless weddings, including my own, there was something deeper and more special about Father Gallo's words tonight. It was as if they meant more than I'd ever before realized. When we said our vows, I kept my gaze on Nick, his dark yet sexy stare, the way his chiseled jaw clenched, and the tightening muscles in his temples.

I handed my flowers to Izzy and took Nick's ring.

My hands were steady as he placed the wedding band on my finger and as I placed the band on his.

Finally, Father Gallo lifted his hands. "Nicolas Ruiz, you may kiss your bride."

Nick's lips quirked. "*My* bride."

"Your bride."

The star-studded sky, ocean breeze, and patio of people disappeared as Nick's lips took mine. I pushed upward on my tiptoes, feeling that tightening low in my stomach. When we finally pulled away, the world around us came back into focus.

"Señora Nick Ruiz," Nick said. "That's now your name."

"It is."

As we turned to face the congregation, I squeezed Nick's hand for support. My sights landed on an older couple sitting in the last row. I wasn't certain how I'd missed them before. I hadn't seen them since Gerardo's funeral.

My parents.

NINETEEN

Nick

"May I be the first," Father Gallo said, "to introduce Señor and Señora Nicolas Ruiz."

The guests stood and clapped.

Liliana's grasp of my hand tightened, alerting me of unexpected alarm. Her glowing smile from a moment earlier was gone, the color drained from her cheeks. I followed her line of vision to the back row of guests. There was a couple present I didn't recognize, but I was certain my wife did. "Are you okay?" I whispered.

It was as if my question pulled Liliana from a spell.

Her soft brown eyes met mine, and her beautiful smile returned. "Of course, I'm your wife."

"Are you able to walk to our reception or should I carry you?"

The sparkle was back. "I can walk."

With her hand in mine, we made our way between the guests as congratulations came from both sides of the aisle. Once inside *el Patrón* and Mia's house, I tugged Liliana to the front of the house, outside into the inner courtyard, trying for a moment of privacy.

"Where are we going?" she asked.

Once outside, I reached for her cheeks and pulled her face toward mine. This was the kiss I wanted to give her during the ceremony. She tasted of mint and spice. Liliana willingly allowed my tongue entrance as hers joined the tango. When I released her, she panted for breath, a smile curling her lips.

"I like your kisses."

"That's good," I said, "I plan on doing that a lot more."

Liliana looked around. Beyond the inner gates, guards patrolled with long guns. Yet within the courtyard, there was a sense of calm. The dark sky was filled with stars, as if God himself approved of our marriage, adding his own twinkling lights.

"Did you bring me out here just to kiss me?" she asked.

"That's one of the reasons."

"What's the other?"

"That couple in the back, they're your parents, aren't they?"

Liliana nodded.

"I don't recall seeing them before."

"You have," she said. "The last time I saw them was Gerardo's funeral."

I scoffed. "Well, sorry, they didn't make an impression on me."

"My father now answers to Reinaldo. I wonder if he made them attend."

"Why would Rei do that?"

"Sofia is here. Jasmine invited her to fly down from Sacramento. I feel like Sofia would have told me my parents were here." She shook her head. "I don't know what to think."

I was trying to recall before the ceremony. Em and I had been in *el Patrón's* office. "I didn't see them enter." I shrugged. "They didn't arrive with Rei and Jasmine."

Liliana feigned a smile. "Do you think we should go back inside for our reception?"

I wiggled my eyebrows. "Or we could skip the reception and go straight to our apartment."

"Ours?"

"*Sí*, Señora Ruiz, you not only have my name, but you have gained a roommate."

"And a new bodyguard."

"*Sí*. However, I think it would be best not to have any live-in help for at least a few days."

"Why is that?"

"Because with the plans I have for us, it would be better if we didn't have an audience."

Liliana tucked her chin.

I reached for it and lifted her face. "You're my wife. You can tell me no."

Her long lashes blinked, revealing her soft suede orbs. "Thank you. I don't think I want to do that. It's good to know I can."

The door to our side opened, warm light spilling onto the pavers. "Hey," Mia said. "There's a party in here for you two. Do you think you'd like to attend?"

"I'm going to kiss my wife one more time," I replied.

Mia smiled and waved before going back into the house.

Our lips met.

"I love you, Liliana. Never forget that."

"I love you too."

With her hand in mine, we walked back into the house. Down the hall we saw the guests mingling around the living room and out onto the patio. However, it was the discussion in *el Patrón's* office that caught my attention, especially at the mention of my wife's name. Liliana and I stopped.

"That's my father," she whispered.

I jutted my chin toward the living room. "Go. I'll find out what this is about."

"No."

I wrinkled my brow. "Did you say no?"

"I did. You just told me I could. I'm not afraid of my father, especially not with you at my side. I want to hear what he's saying to *el Patrón*."

"I really don't want to have to kill him in front of you."

My wife grinned. She actually grinned.

"I trust you to do what's right."

"Okay." I knocked on the partially open door and pushed it inward.

Liliana's mother, Nailea, was sitting in a chair near the window. "Lily," she said softly as we entered. She wasn't my focus.

The discussion involving Socorro Cervantes, Rei, my father, and *el Patrón* garnered our attention. Socorro, turned to us. His expression was less than heartening as he straightened his neck and scanned Liliana and me up and down.

Tugging on Liliana's hand, I moved her partially behind me as I took a step forward. "I'm sensing an issue," I said, puffing my chest.

"Nick," *el Patrón* said, "the Cervanteses were just leaving. I've called Silas to drive them to the airport."

"You're leaving?" Liliana asked.

Socorro's focus was on me. "You think you can marry my daughter without talking to me?"

I nodded. "Yes."

"She's my daughter," he said louder. "When Gerardo married her, he offered compensation for her hand—a bride price. We negotiated." He waved his hand up and down. "You just take her? Is that because she's no longer of value. She's not a virgin." He spat out the last sentence like the words were sour.

Gritting my teeth, I took another step forward. "You stopped being her father after Gerardo was killed. You have no right to make any decisions for her."

"Nailea," he said. "I told you he wouldn't pay for used goods."

Rage roiled through my circulation. I didn't plan or strategize my next move. Within a second or two, I had my knife unsheathed, Socorro's suit coat gathered in my fist, and the tip of my knife at Socorro's throat.

My name was shouted from around the room.

"Rei, you deal with your soldier," *el Patrón* said.

Liliana's mother was now standing. "*El Patrón*, we're sorry. We'll leave."

"How much?" I asked through clenched teeth.

A trickle of blood appeared on Socorro's neck.

"How much did my uncle pay?" I asked again.

Socorro's eyes bulged.

"Fifty thousand," Nailea replied. "Socorro tried for more, but *el Patrón*, Jorge, agreed to fifty thousand."

Liliana gasped. "You sold me to that monster for fifty thousand dollars?"

I pulled my knife an inch away from my father-in-law's flesh. "Leave today. Do not contact my wife again, ever, and I'll pay you one hundred thousand dollars."

"Nick," my wife gasped. "No. He doesn't—they don't deserve your money."

Pushing Socorro backward, he stumbled as I sheathed my knife and turned to Jano. "*El Patrón*, I'd like to pay the Cervanteses one hundred thousand dollars for my wife's hand."

Socorro's expression morphed from fright to a smug smirk.

"Nick," he said. "Socorro is wrong."

"He is," I agreed. "There's no price worthy of Liliana's hand." I turned, meeting my wife's teary gaze and lifted my hand to her. Slowly, she put her hand in mine. I turned back to Jano. "And Cervantes is also wrong that Liliana has no value. My wife is priceless. Please authorize the bride price."

"Are you sure?" my father asked.

I looked him in the eye. We'd disagreed on many things of late. I wasn't confident that he'd have my back. It was my money. His opinion was moot. "Positive," I replied.

"*El Patrón*," my father said, "I support my son's decision."

Jano looked at Rei. "I'll approve the bride price if you take care of other matters in Sacramento."

"*Sí*, it will be done."

Liliana stepped forward. "What will be done?"

It was *el Patrón* who answered. "A soldier does not

enter my home and make demands without consequences."

Socorros's complexion paled. A drop of blood slith-
ered down his neck as his Adam's apple bobbed. I took
a step closer to my father-in-law. "You'll have your
money. You and your wife are dead to us even if Rei
allows you to live. Never darken our lives with your
presence."

There was no doubt he had more to say; however,
with *el Patrón*, his second-in-command, and top lieutenants in attendance, he wisely only nodded.

TWENTY

Liliana

I held my head high as Silas and a guard I didn't recognize entered the crowded office. Mama went to my father's side, her eyes down. As Silas guided them from the room, Mama whispered, "I'm sorry, Lily."

El Patrón's office remained silent until they were gone.

Nick turned to me. "*Tesoro*, are you all right?"

"Why would you offer him that much money?"

"You heard me." Nick's smile curled. "You, Señora Nick Ruiz, are priceless."

"But you didn't have to. *El Patrón* said—"

His lips stopped mine, muting my words and

tenderly kissing me. For a second, I forgot we were in *el Patrón's* office, with the boss, Rei, and my father-in-law, Lieutenant Ruiz. Heat filled my cheeks as I remembered our audience and took a step back.

"I'm sorry about this," I said to everyone. "I told Mia to let them know about the wedding. I thought they might want to..." I shrugged. "I never expected..." I took a ragged breath. "I didn't know about Gerardo's payment."

"The scene is forgotten," Jano said. "My wife, she's worked hard for you to celebrate your wedding."

Nick squeezed my hand. "Let's go see the guests we want to see."

I brushed my cheeks with my fingertips, wondering if I'd ruined the makeup artist's hard work. "I'm probably a mess."

"You're gorgeous."

I wasn't confident about that, but I liked knowing that was the way my husband saw me. He placed his large hand in the small of my back. His touch gave me the confidence to face the other guests. Together we exited *el Patrón's* office.

"There they are," Mia called.

It was the first time I was able to scan our guests. Besides the family members—Ruiz and Roríguez—Celeste, Reina, Luz, and Julia from the apartments were in attendance. They looked stunning, wearing cocktail dresses and high-heeled sandals, and holding flutes of champagne. If anyone in attendance didn't recognize them or know what they did for a living, they would never guess.

I hurried over to the four of them. "I didn't know you'd be here."

"Mia invited us," Julia said.

"A real invitation," Luz added.

They all giggled.

"Am I missing something?" I asked.

"We snuck into Isabella's wedding," Julia said. "With Mia's approval. But this time, she said we could stay." She stood taller. "We're actual guests of *el Patrón*."

"I couldn't be happier to have my friends witness my wedding."

"It was beautiful," Celeste said, "even if you did marry my last hope at a top lieutenant."

It was my turn to laugh. "I never thought I'd be this happy about another marriage."

"It shows," Reina said. "You're glowing."

I felt Nick's presence before his warmth radiated from my back and his large hand wrapped around my waist. "Thank you for joining us," he said to the residents. "I asked Mia to be sure you'd be here." He kissed my cheek. "I know how much you all mean to Liliana."

Craning my neck, I grinned in his direction. "It was your idea?"

"*Sí*. And judging by your smile, it was a good one."

"*Sí, muy buena.*"

"Sorry, ladies, I'm going to steal my wife for a minute."

"I hope you last longer than a minute," Julia said with a grin.

I stifled a giggle as Nick guided me away.

"Have you officially met Joséfina Roríguez?" he asked.

"I saw her at Mia and Jano's wedding, but we didn't speak."

"Come," he said.

Joséfina, Jano and Rei's mother, was a stunning beauty, reminding me of Salma Hayek. Her high cheekbones and long dark hair made her appear too young to be the mother of grown men. Wearing a navy-blue chiffon dress, she was sitting in the living room with Jorge in her arms.

"Señora Roríguez," Nick said.

She looked up, her brown eyes assessing as a smile spread across her lips. "Nick."

"Señora, may I introduce my bride, Liliana Ruiz."

"*El placer es mio.*"

"*Gracias, es un placer conocerte oficialmente.*" I looked down at Jorge. "He's happy to be with his abuela."

"*Sí,* my first grandson. Jasmine's going to have another strong boy. Maybe Mia's next will be a girl."

"Oh, she wouldn't be spoiled at all," I said with a scoff.

Joséfina laughed. "All *ninos* should be spoiled with love."

"They should." I tried not to think of my own parents.

"Congratulations," Jasmine said as she came up to us, her baby bump protruding from her midsection. "Beautiful wedding."

"Thank you."

"Liliana, may I speak with you a moment?"

My gaze went to Nick and back to Jasmine. We were aware of one another, but I couldn't recall a time Jasmine and I spoke privately. Nervously, I followed her out onto the terrace.

"Congratulations again," she said once we were more secluded. Her hand went to her belly, the way many pregnant women's did. "I wanted to personally invite you and Nick to our home for Christmas Eve. It's a tradition with my family, the feast of seven fishes."

"I've never heard of that."

"It's an Italian-American tradition." She scoffed. "I'm not really Italian, but I was raised that way by Dario, and it doesn't feel right not to carry on the tradition with all of our family."

I pressed my lips together. "I'm sorry, Jasmine. I don't think I'm ready to enter your home."

"It was yours first."

I shook my head. "It wasn't a home then."

Jasmine nodded and inhaled. "Before I moved to Sacramento with Reinaldo, there was a coordinated attack on Jano's house and ours. It did a lot of damage. Rei had the house renovated. Maybe you can be there with Nick and make new memories. We really would like the two of you to attend."

Swallowing my emotion, I nodded. "I'll talk with Nick."

Her smile bloomed. "Thank you. That's the most I can hope for. I'm sure you remember, the house is huge. We really do have room for everyone."

"Thank you, Jasmine." I reached out and squeezed her hand. "If Nick isn't needed here, I'll do my best. And thank you for bringing Sofia." I remembered my earlier thought. "Did my parents come down with you and Rei, too?"

"No." She shook her head, a cloud passing over her blue eyes. "I didn't know your parents came. Are they still here?"

"No, they had to leave."

"I'm sorry. I didn't even think of asking them to travel with us. I know Rei has mentioned Socorro from time to time."

Pressing my lips together, I shook my head. "Please don't worry about it."

Her eyes widened. "I could ask Rei to invite them to Christmas Eve."

"Oh no. I wouldn't want them to intrude."

"It's—"

"Please don't," I interrupted. "My father and Nick..." I lowered my voice. "Nick might actually kill him next time, and I think that's the wrong way to spend Christmas Eve or your fish feast."

"Feast of seven fishes," she corrected with a giggle. "You're serious about Nick?"

"Very."

"Okay, noted," Jasmine said. "We will not invite your parents."

"Your invitation is sounding better all the time."

Mia came up to us holding a champagne flute. "Jasmine, I'd offer you a glass, but you and I are in the same boat."

"Damn Roríguez men," Jasmine said with a smile.

Mia turned to me. "Jano told me what happened. Here" —she handed me the flute— "drink up. It's about time to cut the cake so we can begin eating."

"It smells delicious," Jasmine said.

"Viviana and Silas will be with us next week. If you need her to help with the feast of seven fishes, she'd love to."

"You know about that?" I asked.

"Oh, honey," Mia said, "I'm Italian. I know all about it."

Jasmine smiled. "Violeta, our cook, is willing for any and all assistance. Of course, Contessa is an expert when it comes to preparing the traditional meal. She's arriving with Catalina and Ariadna Gia in a couple of days, but I'm sure Violeta will welcome the extra hands if Viviana doesn't mind."

"I'll ask," Mia said. "Now, let's find Nick and cut the cake."

As Mia led me through the people, a petite hand reached out, touching my arm. "Liliana."

My gaze met Maria Ruiz's, my sister-in-law turned mother-in-law. "Maria."

"May we start over?" she asked. "Put our past behind us and begin anew, mother and daughter?"

Emotion suddenly clogged my throat as tears prickled the back of my eyes. "Lieutenant Ruiz told you about my parents."

"*Sí*," she nodded. "It's incomprehensible. My Nick truly loves you, Liliana. I know you've become independent. I think that is something Nick admires. However, if you ever need or want an ear to listen, a shoulder to cry on, or just a hug, know I'm here."

Nibbling my lip, I smiled. "Thank you, Maria. I'm ready to start over."

Nick appeared at my side. "Is everything all right?" His gaze moved from me to his mother and back.

"Everything is wonderful," I said. Turning, I opened my arms.

Maria leaned closer and we embraced. "Welcome, *hija*."

"*Gracias*."

"Mia wants us to cut the cake. The guests are getting restless on champagne and hors d'oeuvres."

The rest of the evening sailed by smoothly. No knives or guns were pulled. The food was delicious.

Nick and I made our way around the crowd, trying to talk to and thank everyone for coming on such short notice. Whenever we'd reunite, he'd wrap his arms around me, kiss me, and tell me he loved me.

It was about nine at night when my husband placed his hand in the small of my back. "Señora Ruiz, shall we go home?"

"Home," I repeated with a smile. I hadn't been back to the apartment since the night José died. Suddenly, I wondered what shape it was in. Had Renata been able to go back and collect her things? "I haven't been back since the night you drove me to the apartments. I don't know if we even have groceries."

Nick's lips quirked and a twinkle came to his eyes. His tone dropped an octave. "Not high on my priority list. Getting you home alone is at the top."

The change in his timbre was all it took to bring back that twisting sensation in my core. "Then let's go home, husband."

TWENTY-ONE

Liliana

"Give those to me."

I handed the keys to Nick. With a mischievous grin, he unlocked the door to our apartment. Before I could register his intention, I was lifted from the floor. I gasped as Nick cradled me against his wide chest.

"Carrying my bride over the threshold."

Framing his cheeks with my palms, I kissed his lips. Once inside the door, he gently lowered me to the floor. It was then I realized someone had been in the apartment. The tree lights were on, sending LED colorful illumination over the marble floor. The disarray from José's death and my sudden exit was gone.

I walked to the fireplace in awe of the stockings hanging there, one with my name and one with Nick's. "How did you do this?"

"It wasn't officially me."

"Who?"

"Mom and Aunt Valentina. They asked what they could do. I knew I wanted to bring you back here, but things have been busy...they said they'd love to get our home arranged."

Maria and Valentina.

I ran my fingers over the stockings. "What about José and Renata's room?"

"Go look."

Nick followed behind as I walked the hallway to the left to their suite. My chest ached as I opened the door, remembering José. When I turned on the light, the room flooded with illumination. The king-sized bed was made. Everything was clean.

"It's ready for our new guards."

My smile dimmed. "I wish I could tell Renata how much I appreciated them and let her know I'm married."

Nick's eyebrows quirked. "Yes, you are." He reached for my hand. "There are fresh groceries in the kitchen. Mom even filled the refrigerator with some of Marcela's specialties." He tugged me closer. "We can honeymoon undisturbed for a day or two."

"I can't believe Maria and Valentina did this." I leaned against his solid chest.

His arms encircled me. "What were the two of you talking about earlier tonight?"

"She asked if we could start over, this time as mother and daughter."

"My dad must have—"

I nodded. "He told her about my parents, but it was more than that. When I married the first time, I was younger than their children. Gerardo expected me to fit in with them as a sister-in-law, but I didn't. I never felt welcomed. I was probably scared to talk to anyone, afraid they'd see how miserable I was."

He kissed my forehead. "He's gone."

My smile returned. "He is, but what Maria said tonight meant a lot to me. And as it happens, I'm currently empty in the mother department."

"Mom sees that I'm happy with you. That makes her happy."

I dropped my forehead to Nick's chest and sighed. Inhaling, I took in his cedar scent and looked up. "I'm happy. I'm truly happy for the first time I can remember."

"Come." He reached for my hand.

We walked back to the living room and past the tree. The lights reflected in the tall windows that led to a small balcony. The city of San Diego twinkled all around us. He led me down the other hallway.

"The last time I walked into this bedroom..." he said.

"You saw me naked."

"No, I didn't. Tonight, I will."

A dozen roses were on my bedside stand. Our blankets were turned back with rose pedals on the pillows and comforter. "Your mom thought of everything."

Nick spun me around by my shoulders. "What am I supposed to do with these bows?"

"There are buttons." A laugh bubbled from my throat. "And I believe there is a row of eye hooks beneath them."

"What the fuck is an eye hook?"

Craning my neck, I saw the determination in his eyes. "You're a smart man, a lieutenant, one of *el Patrón's* best. I think you can figure it out."

"Oh, they're like the clasp on a bra."

I shook my head. "See, I knew you could do it. You're probably very experienced with bra clasps."

He kissed my cheek, my neck, and my shoulder. "I'm not a virgin."

"Neither am I."

His kisses moved lower as he figured out how to undo the row of eye hooks and buttons. Each contact of his lips on my skin sent goose bumps over my arms and legs. Finally, he stood and spun me toward him.

Nick removed the pearl combs from my hair, allowing it to cascade over my shoulders. "This is what I've imagined as I beat off in the shower." He gently teased the spaghetti straps from my shoulders. As with the night he walked in my bedroom, I wasn't wearing a bra.

My silk dress fell to the white rug, a white puddle around my shoes, leaving me in white lace panties. I dropped my arms to my sides.

"You're fucking gorgeous."

My breasts moved as my breathing quickened. I took a step forward. "You've seen me, but I haven't seen you." I pushed the sleeves of his suit jacket from his wide shoulders. Next, I tugged on his white silk tie. My fingers moved over the row of buttons on his shirt as I tugged it from his waist. My hands stilled on the buckle of his belt as memories of seeing the same belt on my desk set off detonations throughout my nervous system.

Looking up through my lashes, I smiled. "I've been following your rule."

Nick reached for the belt and unbuckled it, pulling it from the pant loops, and dropping it to the floor. He kicked off his shoes and removed his pants. Soon we were both dressed accordingly: me in my lace panties and he in black silk boxer briefs.

I stepped out of my shoes, wiggling my toes on the shag rug.

"I want you so fucking bad," he growled, his timbre reverberating through my circulation.

"I want you, too. What you said you did in the shower..."

His grin was back. "I masturbated, Liliana."

I nodded. "I did too, thinking about you." Warmth creeped up my décolletage to my cheeks. "I think I orgasmed."

"You think?"

"I've never done it before."

His dark orbs glistened. "Never?"

Shaking my head, I replied, "Just recently. I liked it."

Nick's smile grew as he backed me toward the large bed. "I promise you'll have many, many more orgasms."

"You sound sure of yourself."

"I'm very sure of myself." He jutted his chin. "Lie back."

I did as he said, scooting from the end of the bed toward the pillows. Nick followed, crawling on all fours. He was a predator, and I was his willing prey. He reached for the waistband of my panties and slid them down my legs. Once in his grasp, he put them to his nose.

"You smell sweet. I knew you would."

He moved up my body, his head dipping at my breasts, his lips capturing each nipple and his tongue teasing the hard buds. Lower and lower his lips moved. I didn't remember lifting my knees or spreading my legs. I was too enthralled with the sensation of his masterful lips. While I didn't remember the movements, I'd done them because as his mouth reached my core, I screamed out.

The sensation was overwhelming. My hips bucked and my thighs tightened to a vise grip of his head. No matter what my movements, Nick continued with his lips and tongue. I reached for the sheets to keep myself from floating away as he wound my insides taut, ready to spin out of control.

"Oh God, Nick."

He splayed his fingers over my pelvis, holding me in place. It was as he licked and nipped my clit that I yelled out. There weren't words. It wasn't a known language, yet the sounds filled the bedroom—Nick's slurps and hums and my wanton sounds—until the winding snapped. A tremor swept through my body as explosions like I'd never known detonated beneath my flesh.

Nick moved up, wedging himself between my legs. "One," he said with a smirk.

I blinked trying to recover. "I've never...I feel like a ragdoll."

"Oh, we're not done."

"I think..."

Nick reached lower, pulling down his boxer briefs. The weight and length of his penis probed my stomach.

I opened my eyes, staring into his.

"Tell me to stop and I'll stop. I'll go into the bathroom and beat this bad boy into submission."

Shaking my head, I wiggled, lifting my knees higher. "Don't stop."

His expression morphed.

Relief.

Jubilation.

Elation.

"I love you, Liliana."

Lifting my hands to his shoulders, I caressed his warm skin. "I love you, Nick. I want you inside me."

As the head of his penis pushed between my folds, my body wanted to revolt, to keep him from doing what I'd just asked for him to do. I kept my eyes open, staring at the man with me. Seeing his handsome face, smelling his cedar scent, and feeling his heat and strength. This was my new husband, a man I trusted completely. The man who believed in my worth.

"Are you all right?"

I nodded with a smile. "I am."

A gasp came from my lips as he pressed inside me. Nick was definitely more man than my first husband.

He stilled. "Liliana."

"You're supposed to keep moving."

His laugh filled the air. "I know what to do. I am checking on you."

My eyes opened wide. "I've never felt so full."

He kissed me as his hips began to thrust. No longer was the air filled with only my wanton noises, but Nick added the bass clef to our melody. Despite his obvious size, the sensation of him pulling nearly out and pushing deep inside was surprisingly pleasant. No, more than pleasant. It was erotic.

I ran my fingertips over his shoulders and back, feeling the way his muscles tightened and released, tightened and released. The buildup to this orgasm was slower, the chugging of a freight train up a hill. Tighter and tighter my body wound. The crest was nearby. Nick's thrusts came harder and longer. We reached the other side of the hill, and the train sped down the track. His growl echoed throughout the air as he filled me to overflowing.

For a few moments, we lay there, together in the tangled sheets, waiting for our breathing to return to regular. Finally, Nick arched his back, looking down at me. "Are you...?"

Arching my neck, I kissed his lips. "Two."

He grinned. "Never before?"

"Just the one time by myself. But honestly, it was something but nothing compared to these."

He pulled out.

I immediately missed the closeness.

Nick rolled from the bed and stood. Our juices glistened on his still-erect cock.

Holy shit.

I stifled a laugh.

"What's so funny, *señora*?"

"I'm glad I didn't see you before...you're...well, it would have scared me."

Nick smirked. "I fit inside you perfectly. A puzzle

meant to be together." He disappeared into the bathroom. When he returned, he was wearing his boxer briefs, and he had a warm washcloth. "Let me."

I flung back the sheet, revealing my nakedness. There was something about the way he was tending to me that made my heart swell. Soon, he was back in bed, his arm wrapped around me. My head was on his shoulder. I lifted my face to see him better. "Nick, I really am happy."

"That's all I want."

"Jasmine asked if we'd go to her house on Christmas Eve. A feast of fishes."

"Seven fishes."

I playfully slapped his chest. "How does everyone know about this but me?"

"You haven't had the honor of experiencing a Luciano Christmas tradition." He rubbed gentle circles on my back. "If you don't want to go to their house, I'll tell *el Patrón* I'll watch over our territory while he's up north."

"Does he need you to do that?"

"Why?"

I inhaled. "Because if you can go, I'd like to go." My smile returned. "Like Maria said, we're starting over." I kissed his chest. "We're making new memories."

CHAPTER

TWENTY-TWO

Nick

I wasn't certain what to expect when it came to Liliana and intimacy. I don't just mean sex. She'd been through a difficult time with Uncle Gerardo. While I didn't know all the details, I could imagine, and doing so made me wish I'd been present when *el Patrón* carried out his sentence.

Her honesty was refreshing. She surprised me at every turn.

The morning after our wedding, we showered together, cleaning and touching one another. Heavy steam hung in the air. With her hands splayed as she faced the tile, she peered at me over her shoulder. "Talk to me, Nick. Keep reminding me it's you."

My cock hardened at her plea. "You're fucking amazing, Liliana." Scooping her wet hair, I peppered her neck with kisses before slipping my cock inside her. Her warm pussy clamped around me like a vise. I continued whispering in her ear, reminding her she was now mine, loved, and cherished. I pumped and thrust until her body tensed and her voice echoed throughout the bathroom.

Later, with Liliana wearing only a robe and me in my boxers, we sat on the balcony. Overlooking the city, we drank coffee and talked. I'd never seen a woman as self-assured, absolutely stunning with her wet hair and no makeup. When she'd move, her robe would gape open just enough to offer me a peek of her pert breasts, deep-red areolas, and tight nipples.

Throughout the day and night, we christened our home in a way we wouldn't be able to do once a new bodyguard moved in with us. Nothing was off-limits from the kitchen counter to the dining room table, and over the arm of the sofa. No matter the location, or whether our eyes stayed locked on one another, I continued to speak, to reassure her that this was real.

After the sofa, I smacked her round ass, just to see my handprint. Liliana only craned her neck and smiled. "Am I being naughty? Is sex on the couch against your rules?"

"No, *tesoro*. I just wanted to see my handprint on your sexy ass."

Finally, Monday morning, we ventured out. I drove

my wife to the apartments, walking her inside. Celeste and Reina were awaiting her arrival.

"Look at her smile," Celeste said. She winked at me. "You must be doing something right."

I hardened my expression. "I'm still your lieutenant."

"*Sí*, Lieutenant Ruiz."

My smile returned as I kissed Liliana. "I'm sending Diego here today. If you need to go anywhere, he'll drive you."

The most beautiful shade of pink filled her cheeks. "I guess we forgot to discuss the whole new body-guard thing."

"*Sí*, we used our time together doing and saying more important things." I leaned down, giving her one more kiss. "Love you."

"I love you, too."

As soon as I was back in the car, I called Em and asked him to catch me up on all things Roríguez cartel. He said he'd call me back as soon as he dropped Isabella off at the apartments. I took a longer route to *el Patrón's,* wanting to put some eyes on the street. Taking two days off was something I'd never before done. I wanted to be sure I knew what was happening when I walked into Jano's office.

Traffic was unsurprisingly heavy near the ship-yard. I drove south to the warehouse. There were few cars parked within the large structure. Climbing the steps, I went inside. A few falcons were present—the men that were the eyes and ears on the street. I took their reports, learning the streets over the last few nights were typical weekend incidents. A few gang fights, a couple shootings, and an incident with masked law enforcement. All of our men were accounted for.

I was heading back to my car when Em called.

"*Hola*," I said as I answered.

"I saw Liliana when I dropped Isabella off. She seems happy."

A smile curled my lips. That's what I wanted, for her to be happy in a way others saw her happiness. "What have I missed over the last few days?"

Getting in my car, Em's voice played through the speakers. "Cabezõn's been quiet. Too quiet. Your father oversaw Wanderland while you were on your honeymoon. He has security footage of two men he believes are with Cabezõn."

"How the fuck did they get in Wanderland?"

"Rei's going through the footage. We'll find out what bouncer they got past."

And then we'll bring him in the office for questioning. "I stopped by the warehouse," I said, "and talked to some of our falcons. The usual shit is happening on the streets, but nothing that stands out."

"There's something else," Em said. "I should probably let Jano tell you, but damn, I think you should know."

"*Qué pasó?*"

TWENTY-THREE

Liliana

Celeste and Reina sprinted to my office as soon as Nick left the building. "Are you truly as happy as you look?" Reina asked.

I nodded, my smile growing larger. "I'm happier than I ever imagined I could be."

Celeste feigned a frown. "I should have made a play for him sooner."

"You missed a good one," I replied, sitting in my desk chair. "I think I gave up on the idea of ever being loved."

Reina sat in the chair near my desk while Celeste leaned against the wall. "Liliana, you've been loved," Reina said. "All the residents adore you. Obviously so does Mia and damn, girl, *el Patrón* walked you down the freakin' aisle."

"He did." I recalled how he gave me a last chance to back out of the marriage.

"Did that piss off your father?" she asked.

My thoughts went to my parents, hampering my joy. "I no longer have a father or mother."

Celeste tilted her head. "What happened?"

"I don't want to get into it." I inhaled, sitting taller. "I'd rather think about Nick."

Celeste's eyes shone with understanding. "Your wedding was beautiful. The terrace, sunset, lights…it was magical."

"It was as perfect as it could be." I met their gazes. "Thank you for coming."

"We wouldn't have missed it for the world," Reina said.

"I'm sorry I wasn't the one to invite you. Everything happened at once." I remembered the rumor the day after the apartments were attacked. "Have you heard anything else about Cabezõn's men. Were some captured?"

Celeste went to my office door and peeked her head out. Quietly, she closed the door. "I would think you'd know all about it."

I shook my head. "Oh, if you mean because of Nick, we stayed off the radar all weekend."

Reina's eyebrows danced. "Off the radar. Hmm, sounds good to me."

"Well," Celeste said, "Saturday night, two of Cabezõn's soldiers came into the club asking questions."

"There's a room downstairs in the basement of Wanderland," Reina said, speaking as if she was divulging cartel secrets. "Those who heard them said they were trying to find out where the cartel would take their men for questioning."

"Did they cause problems?" I asked.

"Lieutenant Ruiz, Nick's father, was overseeing the club. Once he heard they were on the premises, he had them removed."

"How would they learn about the interrogation room?" I asked.

Celeste shrugged. "Mia came by here on Sunday. All the women swear they haven't told a soul."

"She believed you. Right?"

Reina nodded. "I think Nick's father thought blaming the whores was the way to go."

"I'm so glad," Celeste said, "we have Mia." She looked at me. "And you and Izzy."

A knock interrupted our gossip.

Celeste went to the door, turning the knob. Her smile grew. "Speak of the devil." She opened the door wider, revealing Em and Isabella. "We'll get back to the front office."

Reina and Celeste exited as Em and Isabella entered.

"Welcome back," Izzy said with a grin. "Look at you."

"Tell me to kick Nick's ass," Em said, "and I will."

My laugh bubbled from my throat. "Please don't."

"Damn," Em replied, "I guess I'll have to find someone else to kill today."

Izzy playfully pushed against his muscular arm. "Stop it. You're not as deadly as you pretend."

"Oh, I'm deadly, just not around my beautiful naïve wife."

"I'm not naïve."

Em kissed her cheek. "Horace will be here soon. I'll see you tonight at home."

After Em left, I asked, "Is Sofia still at your house?"

"She's going back north today."

"Oh," I said disappointedly. "I wish I would have been able to see her for longer."

Izzy's blue eyes widened. "I'm sure she understood that you and Nick had more important things to do."

Warmth filled my cheeks. "It must seem so weird to look at our relationship from the outside, but even though I've known Nick for years, I feel like we're getting to know one another all over again. He talks."

"Yes, I've heard him do that."

"No," I said with a scoff. "He talks and listens. We talked about so many things. Gerardo...he didn't share."

"Maybe it's generational. Em talks and listens."

She shrugged. "I think Andrés does too. I'm not sure my father does."

"I feel at ease with Nick, not like I'm constantly walking on eggshells."

"That's the way it's supposed to be. I think I fell in love with Em in Mia's office. He was showing me Mia's programs, but he wasn't all bossy and mansplaining. He actually listened when I spoke. My father never did."

"It sounds like we got two of the good ones."

"Are you going to Rei and Jasmine's for the feast of seven fishes?"

I giggled. "I looked that up over the weekend."

"Oh, you had time?" Her eyebrows danced. "I assumed you were constantly on your back?"

"No," I said, the heat coming back to my cheeks. "Sometimes I was standing or bent over." The heat radiated down my neck. "Once, I was even on top."

Izzy's laugh filled my office. "Good for you. And you still had time to research the feast of seven fishes and learn that it's an ancient Catholic tradition. My family, the Lucianos, always celebrated it. We used to go to my aunt and uncle's house in the Ozarks. Then after Dario married Catalina, the celebration moved to his home. The big question is if Aunt Arianna will go to Sacramento."

"She's Mia's mother, right?"

"Right, and Dario and Dante's."

"Why wouldn't she come?" I asked.

"She's never approved of Jasmine."

My mouth went slack. "I didn't know that."

"Jasmine moved in with Dario when she was really young. I honestly don't remember a time when she wasn't there." Izzy's smile dimmed. "We were horrible to her on the few occasions we saw her. She and her sister, Josie, lived with Dario. Uncle Vincent and Aunt Arianna didn't approve, so none of us did, even Mia."

"Mia? She and Jasmine seemed fine. They were talking at the wedding."

"They've come a long way. I've apologized to Jasmine. I asked her at your wedding if she invited Aunt Arianna, and she said she did. All I can say is Jasmine is a better person than my aunt ever was."

"But you don't think your aunt will come?"

"I think if she does, it's because Dario made her."

"Her son."

Izzy sat taller. "Her capo dei capi."

"Oh, poor Jasmine."

"Are you going?" Izzy asked.

"Now, I want to go to be there for Jasmine."

"Yeah, I feel the same way."

TWENTY-FOUR

Nick

"What the actual fuck?" I asked as I entered *el Patrón's* office. "Why didn't you call me?"

"Don't question me," Jano said. "I'm in charge." He sent a dark, chastising stare toward Em and back to me. "You weren't supposed to know about it until you arrived." He stood. "I decided you weren't needed in the decision making."

"He's my father-in-law."

"Was. Your bride payment is in limbo. You offered it to Socorro. He's no longer in need of money. I was waiting to talk to you, to find out if you want it to go to Nailea."

"Fuck." I sighed as I fell back into a chair across from Jano's desk. "You were sure of the intelligence?"

El Patrón nodded and sat. "After the wedding, Rei went with Em to pay a visit to our two guests in the basement of Wanderland."

"And they confirmed Socorro was their source?"

Jano templed his fingers and nodded. "They did, but Rei later confirmed it. If we'd known earlier that night, you could have killed him right here."

"How did Socorro know about the apartments?"

"Rei thinks he was the source. He remembered telling Socorro what a good job Liliana was doing."

"Fuck, at least there's no big conspiracy."

Jano replied, "Rei wrongfully thought Socorro would give a shit about his daughter."

"When Rei returned to Sacramento," Em began, "he called Socorro in for a meeting. He told him it was about the bride price. I wasn't in here for the excitement, but Socorro had to know he was on borrowed time after making a scene in *el Patrón's* office after your wedding."

"He thought he'd won," I said. "He wanted cash, and I offered him twice as much as Gerardo."

"Smug," Jano replied. "I ordered Rei to show him the wrong of his ways. I meant punishment. That was before we learned he has been working with Cabezõn."

"I can't believe he was so fucking dumb to come here."

Jano leaned onto his elbows on his desk. "He's of the generation that think they're so much smarter than we are." He nodded. "Speaking of that generation, I was pleased that Nicolas agreed with your offer of the bride price."

"I was too," I admitted.

"He did well at Wanderland the other night," Jano said. "Cabezõn's men were looking for our guests. There's no way to question Socorro. I wonder if he also told them about our interrogation room."

I was trying to wrap my head around the revelation. "Socorro gave Cabezõn info on the apartments knowing his daughter could be caught in the crosshairs."

"*Sí*," Jano said. "The man's a pig."

"At the meeting," Em said, "in Rei's office, Rei demanded Socorro's phone. Socorro didn't want to give it up, but as we all know, Rei can be persuasive. He found evidence of Socorro's communication with Cabezõn. Socorro even bragged to him about your bride payment."

I stood, clenching my teeth. "I fucking should have killed him." I turned to Jano. "What will happen to Nailea?"

El Patrón leaned back. "Liliana wasn't guilty when Gerardo was."

"Back then, she was a scared child. Nailea isn't.

She's a grown woman. She knew, when they arrived at the wedding, her husband's plans to try to extort money off the daughter they'd abandoned." My mind was reeling. "Liliana was protected by the cartel. If Nailea isn't, what do you suspect will happen to her?"

"There's a chance Cabezõn will take her in," Jano said. "She's in her early forties and not bad looking. She has a few good years of work in her."

Cabezõn's whores.

"And if Roríguez protects her?" I asked.

"To be protected, she'll need to remarry."

A smile came to my lips. "She'll be required to marry a man she may or may not know."

"*Sí*, a soldier."

"Be sure she knows he's not paying a bride price for her," I said. "I need to tell Liliana about her father. He was a piece of shit, but he was still her father."

"The bride price?" Jano asked.

"Give it to Mia for the apartments."

El Patrón nodded.

TWENTY-FIVE

Liliana

It had been a few days since Nick informed me of my father's crimes against the cartel. While the news was shocking, I barely grieved. I'd done that years ago when my parents chose to not support me. I was over the five stages of grief, or I should say I was at the final stage—acceptance. Nick showed me what love truly can be. It may have been a lonely road getting to where I was, but it was worth it.

The SUV carrying *el Patrón*, Emiliano, Isabella, Nick, and I stopped in front of Jasmine and Rei's home. The feast of seven fishes was to happen later tonight. Mia, Jorge, Silas, and Viviana traveled north a day earlier. As others got out of the vehicle, Nick reached for my hand. "We can back out. We'll just stay in the SUV and go back to the airport."

I loved how concerned Nick was. "It would be silly to fly from San Diego to change my mind at the last minute."

My chest expanded as I took a deep breath. Jasmine told me that Rei had done some remodeling, but the exterior front looked very similar to how it had the last time I was here.

"*Tesoro*, remember my rule," Nick whispered as we got out of the vehicle.

Shivering in the slightly cooler climate, my eyes went to the cobblestone driveway. I remembered how difficult it was to walk in high heels on the uneven surface. Yet that was what was required of me as the lady of the house. Today, I wore ballet flats. The dichotomy of the past and the present was showcased in everything from my shoes to the man at my side.

"It looks the same," I said.

Nick peered up at the monstrosity of a house. "We're going house hunting after the holidays."

I spun toward him. "Why?"

"Because you used to live in this and now, we're in an apartment."

"No."

His smile quirked up on one side. "You keep saying that."

"You said I could." My cheeks rose. "I've just not said it when you expected me to."

He laid his hand in the small of my back. "Who are you?"

"I'm your wife, Señora Nick Ruiz."

I looked up, seeing Jasmine standing at the door. Her long red hair was pulled back, and her arms were crossed above her growing midsection. "It's warmer inside," she called.

Together, Nick and I climbed the steps. Jasmine wrapped me in a hug. "Thank you for joining us."

"Once I researched the feast of seven fishes, I couldn't wait to experience it."

She ushered us inside.

I gasped. The interior was completely different than I recalled. While the marble floor was the same, the walls were painted a soft gray. The furnishings no longer resembled a museum but looked elegant and homey. "The inside...it's actually homey." I turned toward the front sitting room. While it was filled with familiar faces, I noticed that the grand piano was gone. "And the piano is gone."

"We had it moved to Joséfina's wing. She plays. Neither Rei nor I do. Do you?"

"No," I answered with a grin.

"Nick," Rei called, luring my husband back toward where Gerardo's office used to be.

"Are you going to be all right?" he asked with concern.

I reached for Jasmine's arm. "I'll be good."

She patted my hand. "Let me show you what Rei had done out back."

My eyes were taking in all the improvements. "Even the artwork has changed. It used to be so cold in here."

"Rei did a lot before we married. Since then, he encouraged me to make the house more like us. José-fina has helped."

"You've done a fabulous job."

We stopped at the wall of floor-to-ceiling windows. "The pool."

Jasmine smiled. "The long lap pool was impractical for children. Rei had it removed, and this new pool installed. See the large shallow area?"

"With stone sunchairs."

"Yes," she said. "I love reading out there. And one day José will be playing in the shallow end."

"José," I repeated, thinking of my bodyguard.

"We found out we're having a boy. If the baby was a girl, I wanted to name her Josie after my sister. José is the masculine version—Joséph."

"That's beautiful. I'm sure your sister would be honored."

"Dario's mother won't approve." She lifted her chin. "And I don't give a shit."

"Did she come? Is she here?"

"She's here. If it wasn't for Ariadna Gia, she'd be totally miserable." Jasmine laughed. "I know you have reason to hate this home, but Rei has made me feel like a queen in a castle. I couldn't be happier here with him and Joséfina...and a million guards and staff." She laughed again. "Even the wicked Luciano witch can't refuse my invitation."

I took her in, sensing her confidence. It was my turn to laugh. "Good for you."

"Let's go join the others," Jasmine said.

She led me toward the dining room. Never in my memory had the mammoth room looked so inviting. It was always cold when there were only two people dining. Now, a giant table was set. I started to count the chairs.

"Twenty-eight in the main dining room," Jasmine said, "and more in the back."

We entered the kitchen that led to a large sunroom, both filled with women. I saw Isabella with her sisters and cousins. She'd told me how excited she was to see them. I recognized Noemi, Marisa, Aria, and Cenzi from Isabella and Em's wedding. My smile grew when I saw Sofia in the kitchen standing by Lola, Valentina's cook.

"Sofia," I said, going closer.

"Lily. I'm so glad you're here."

"It's a little weird, isn't it?"

My friend shrugged. "It was weird when you and Dad were here. It hadn't felt like home after Mom died. I'm glad for the house that Rei and Jasmine have made it a home again."

Inhaling the delicious aromas, I nodded. "Love makes a home."

"Did you see what they did to the pool?"

"It will be perfect for their baby next summer."

"He'll be a little too small to swim next summer, but in the future…"

A few hours later, I was seated at Nick's side as *el Patrón* stood, asking for the blessing. His and Mia's seats were near the head of the table with Rei, Jasmine, Dario Luciano, Catalina, Dante and Camila. We all quieted.

Jano looked out over the crowd. "Our alliance continues to endure. To another year of prosperity, health, and wealth."

Dario stood, lifting his glass of wine. "The Luciano famiglia concurs."

Glasses clinked in agreement around the table. Out of the corner of my eye, I saw that even Arianna, Dario and Dante's mother, lifted her glass. Maybe holiday miracles truly happened.

EPILOGUE~

Nick

Four months later

I wake with my body twisted with Liliana's. Her breathing rhythmically raised and lowered her breasts. Her back was to my front; her round ass tucked against me. My arm surrounded her protectively, and our legs were intertwined. Soft hair tickled my nose as my cock increased in size exponentially at her proximity.

Remembering her request from the morning after our wedding, I kissed her hair and spoke. "*Buenos dias, tesoro.*"

Her fine ass wiggled against my erection as her hum filled the air. "Morning," she replied groggily. "Does your cock ever take a break?"

"Not when I'm around you."

Reaching back with her hand she fisted my erection, running her fist up and down before situating me between her folds. "Oh," she purred, as we became one.

I could blame it on the early morning, or the fact my wife was so fucking tight, but I didn't last as long as I had the night before. As I pulled out of her warm, wet heaven, Liliana rolled in my arms, bringing us face-to-face. Her small breasts pressed against my chest, and her smile radiated from ear to ear.

"I think that's my favorite way to wake," she said before brushing my lips with hers.

"And fall asleep."

She cuddled closer. "Can we just spend today in bed? I have a few days off before my mid-terms. I'm tired of studying."

"I'd love to, but..."

Liliana grinned. "There's always a but..."

Reaching down, I pinched her fine ass. "That's the only butt I care about. Today's Jorge's first birthday party."

Her eyes opened wide. "Oh, how could I forget that? And Jasmine and Rei will be there with José."

I ran my finger over her cheek, pushing away rogue hairs. "Does the baby's name remind you of José Pérez?"

She shrugged. "I mean, many people have the same name. On Christmas Eve, Jasmine explained that

Jos is the masculine version of her sister's name, Josie. She and Rei named him after Jasmine's sister."

"I didn't know that."

Liliana sat up, the sheet slipping from her tantalizing body. "Oh, there's something the great Lieutenant Ruiz doesn't know."

Leaning inward, I sucked one of her nipples.

"Nick," she shrieked.

I laughed. "It was either that or slap your ass. Your breast was closer."

"I wasn't breaking your rule."

My eyebrows danced. "What can I say? I like being naughty even when you're being nice."

"I love you."

"I love you, too."

Thank you for reading NAUGHTY AND NICE. If you've read the Brutal Vows series, I hope you enjoyed catching up with the whole gang. If this was your first experience with the Luciano / Roríguez alliance, I hope you'll go back to the beginning. Each of our couples had a story to tell.

Dario and Catalina – NOW AND FOREVER

Aléjandro and Mia – TILL DEATH DO US PART

Dante and Camila –BOUND BY A PROMISE

Reinaldo and Jasmine – QUEENS AND MONSTERS

Emiliano and Isabella – TO HAVE AND TO HOLD

STANDALONE ROMANTIC THRILLER:

FEAR OF FLAMES

October 2025

STANDALONE ROMANTIC SUSPENSE:

DEFENDING LOVE

June 2025

BRUTAL VOWS:

NOW AND FOREVER

May 2024

TILL DEATH DO US PART

June 2024

BOUND BY A PROMISE

October 2024

QUEENS AND MONSTERS

January 2025

TO HAVE AND TO HOLD

March 2025

NAUGHTY AND NICE - A Brutal Vows Holiday Novella

November 2025

SINCLAIR DUET:

REMEMBERING PASSION

September 2023

REKINDLING DESIRE

October 2023

ROYAL REFLECTIONS SERIES:

RUTHLESS REIGN

November 2022

RESILIENT REIGN

January 2023

RAVISHING REIGN

April 2023

RELEVANT REIGN

June 2023

DEVIL'S SERIES (Duet):

DEVIL'S DEAL

May 2021

ANGEL'S PROMISE

June 2021

SPARROW WEBS

WEB OF SIN:

SECRETS

October 2018

LIES

December 2018

PROMISES

January 2019

TANGLED WEB:

TWISTED

May 2019

OBSESSED

July 2019

BOUND

August 2019

WEB OF DESIRE:

SPARK

Jan. 14, 2020

FLAME

February 25, 2020

ASHES

April 7, 2020

DANGEROUS WEB:

Prequel: "Danger's First Kiss"

DUSK

November 2020

DARK

January 2021

DAWN

February 2021

THE INFIDELITY SERIES:

BETRAYAL

Book #1

October 2015

CUNNING

Book #2

January 2016

DECEPTION

Book #3

May 2016

ENTRAPMENT

Book #4

September 2016

FIDELITY

Book #5

January 2017

THE CONSEQUENCES SERIES:

CONSEQUENCES

(Book #1)

August 2011

TRUTH

(Book #2)

October 2012

CONVICTED

(Book #3)

October 2013

REVEALED

(Book #4)

Previously titled: Behind His Eyes Convicted: The Missing Years

June 2014

BEYOND THE CONSEQUENCES

(Book #5)

January 2015

RIPPLES **(Consequences stand-alone)**

October 2017

CONSEQUENCES COMPANION READS:

BEHIND HIS EYES-CONSEQUENCES

January 2014

BEHIND HIS EYES-TRUTH

March 2014

~

STAND ALONE MAFIA THRILLER:

PRICE OF HONOR

Available Now

~

STAND-ALONE YA ROMANTIC THRILLER:

ON THE EDGE

May 2022

~

TALES FROM THE DARK SIDE SERIES:

INSIDIOUS

(All books in this series are stand-alone erotic thrillers)

Released October 2014

~

ALEATHA'S LIGHTER ONES:

PLUS ONE

Stand-alone fun, sexy romance

May 2017

ANOTHER ONE

Stand-alone fun, sexy romance

May 2018

ONE NIGHT

Stand-alone, sexy contemporary romance

September 2017

A SECRET ONE

Prequel to MY ALWAYS ONE

April 2018

MY ALWAYS ONE

Stand-Alone, sexy friends to lovers contemporary romance

July 2021

*QUINTESSENTIALLY THE ONE

Stand-alone, small-town, second-chance, secret baby
contemporary romance

July 2022

*ONE KISS

Stand-alone, small-town, best friend's sister,
grump/sunshine contemporary romance.

July 2023

*ONE STRING

Second-chance, enemies-to-lovers, fake-date, little-sister's-best-friend, forbidden, stand-alone contemporary romance

July 2024

*All Riverbend interconnected stories

INDULGENCE SERIES:

UNEXPECTED

August 2018

UNCONVENTIONAL

January 2018

UNFORGETTABLE

October 2019

UNDENIABLE

August 2020

ABOUT THE AUTHOR

Visit Aleatha's store to purchase e-books, signed books, and store exclusive items.

Aleatha Romig is a New York Times, Wall Street Journal, and USA Today bestselling author who lives in Indiana, USA. She has raised three children with her high school sweetheart and husband of over thirty years. Before she became a full-time author, she worked days as a dental hygienist and spent her nights writing. Now, when she's not imagining mind-blowing twists and turns, she likes to spend her time with her family and friends. Her other pastimes include reading and creating heroes/anti-heroes who haunt your dreams!

Aleatha impresses with her versatility in writing. She released her first novel, CONSEQUENCES, in August of 2011. CONSEQUENCES, a dark romance, became a bestselling series with five novels and two companions released from 2011 through 2015. The compelling and epic story of Anthony and Claire Rawlings has graced more than half a million e-readers. Her first stand-alone smart, sexy thriller INSIDIOUS was next. Then Aleatha released the five-novel INFIDELITY series, a romantic suspense saga, that took the reading world by storm, the final book landing on three of the top bestseller lists. She ventured into traditional publishing with Thomas and Mercer. Her books INTO THE LIGHT and AWAY FROM THE DARK were published through this mystery/thriller publisher in 2016.

In the spring of 2017, Aleatha again ventured into a different genre with her first fun and sexy stand-alone romantic comedy with the USA Today bestseller PLUS ONE. She continued the "Ones" series with additional standalones, ONE NIGHT, ANOTHER ONE, MY ALWAYS ONE, QUINTESSENTIALLY THE ONE, ONE KISS, and ONE STRING.

If you like fun, sexy, novellas that make your heart pound, try her "Indulgence series" with UNCONVENTIONAL. UNEXPECTED, UNFORGETTABLE, and UNDENIABLE.

In 2018 Aleatha returned to her dark romance roots with SPARROW WEBS. And continued with the mafia romance DEVIL'S DUET, and most recently her Brutal Vows series.

You may find all Aleatha's titles on her website.

Aleatha is a "Published Author's Network" member of the Romance Writers of America and PEN America. She is represented by SBR Media and Dani Sanchez with Wildfire Marketing.

www.ingramcontent.com/pod-product-compliance
Lightning Source LLC
Chambersburg PA
CBHW072127300726
48975CB00003B/957